THE HOUSE IN
POPLAR
WOOD

ALSO BY K. E. ORMSBEE

The Water and the Wild
The Doorway and the Deep
The Current and the Cure

THE HOUSE IN
POPLAR
WOOD

K. E. ORMSBEE

chronicle books · san francisco

Library of Congress Cataloging-in-Publication Data available.

ISBN 978-1-4521-4986-8

Manufactured in China.

MIX
Paper from
responsible sources
FSC™ C101537
FSC
www.fsc.org

Design by Amelia Mack.
Typeset in Hightower.

Page vii, "You cannot put a fire out,"
The Complete Poems of Emily Dickinson by
Emily Dickinson. Boston: Little Brown, 1924.

10 9 8 7 6 5 4 3 2 1

Chronicle Books LLC
680 Second Street
San Francisco, California 94107

Chronicle Books—we see things differently.
Become part of our community at www.chroniclekids.com.

to VIRGINIA KATE CARROLL—
keeper of memories,
lover of autumn,
friend

You cannot put a fire out;
A thing that can ignite
Can go, itself, without a fan
Upon the slowest night.

You cannot fold a flood
And put it in a drawer,—
Because the winds would find it out,
And tell your cedar floor.

EMILY DICKINSON

PROLOGUE

It was an ordinary day at Poplar House.

It began, as most ordinary days do, with breakfast.

·|·

Felix Vickery fixed himself porridge, with neither sugar nor butter to flavor the oats.

·|·

Lee Vickery ate his mother's fresh-fried country ham, with a mug of hot apple cider on the side.

·|·

Then, as on all ordinary days, the two brothers saw to their morning chores.

·|·

Felix fetched a brass pot from its perch and filled it with water from the tap. He placed it on the stove and switched on the gas flame.

•|•

Lee trudged to the canning room, opening the door with a skeleton key. There were jars there to be labeled and put away.

•|•

The water boiled, and Felix was ready: In went five rosemary sprigs, followed by the juice of two lemons and half a lime. He stirred the broth well with a wooden spoon.

"Felix!" his father called from down the hall.

"Five more minutes!" Felix called back.

Broths took time to brew. It was one thing to prescribe them, but another to bring them to life.

•|•

"Lee!" his mother called from the parlor.

Lee was finishing his work on the last of the jars—a green ribbon, knotted in a tidy bow.

"Nearly done," he said, scribbling a date and category on the label.

His mother often reminded him that it was easier to write these labels *before* attaching them to their jars; Lee often forgot.

Today, the label read *Remember.*

There were far fewer *Remember*s than *Forget*s.

Reminding and forgetting. That was Lee's life at Poplar House. Reminding and forgetting, siphoning and canning.

Lee placed the jar upon its proper shelf.

"Sealed tight?" asked his mother, seeing him to the front door.

"Sealed tight," Lee replied.

The alternative was disastrous. Memories were fragile things, and far more priceless than jams or preserves. Should one escape, it would evaporate into nothing at all, or worse yet, find its way into another's mind.

•|•

"Brewed right?" asked Felix's father, taking the bowl of broth from his son.

"Brewed right," Felix replied.

It was an everyday question, but an ever-important one.

The broth meant healing. It meant a tomorrow, instead of a never-again. So Felix brewed well and then carried the broth to the examination room.

Today's patient was an old woman with tangled gray hair and half her teeth missing. She drank down the concoction of citrus and rosemary, boiled and stirred to specification. Felix watched as her pale face turned rosier and her dulled eyes filled with life.

As Felix's father helped the woman down, Felix thought of the many patients before her who had lain upon that examination table and never gotten back up. Endings, rather than healings—there had been more than Felix could count.

Healing and ending, brewing and watching. That was Felix's life at Poplar House.

•|•

Chores completed, Lee left the house for school. He walked slow, aiming his boots at orange, crunchable leaves. There was music in his left ear—a song, hummed soft and low, familiar to him. Memory hummed it often on her ramblings through the wood.

The song told Lee he was not alone. He belonged somewhere, and to someone, just the way he liked it.

•|•

Chores completed, Felix stood on the back steps of Poplar House. He watched at a distance, taking in a scene by halves: through his left eye he saw his father, and through his right he saw only a gentleman, dressed in black. The two men were shaking hands in the pink morning sun.

The handshake told Felix he would never be alone. He belonged somewhere, to someone, whether he liked it or not.

1
FELIX

THE LAST DAY of October was creeping into Poplar House. It came through fissures in the gables and mite-sized holes in the floorboards, bringing with it the scent of burnt oak branches.

It was Halloween, and for Felix Vickery, it was the warmest day of the year.

All autumn long, Felix had worn gloves to bed and woken to a fringe of frost on his lashes. Even in the summertime, when the wood outside grew drunk on sunshine and the whole of Boone Ridge gasped for lawn sprinklings and fresh popsicles—even then, a dank chill remained in the house. Even in August, Felix wore long pajamas to bed.

That was the way of it, when you shared a house with Death. Not that most patients believed in *Death*. Though rumors skittered through Boone Ridge and the mining towns tucked farther toward the mountains—rumors of another presence in the house—visitors believed only what was written on the plaque above Poplar House's east-end door, which read VINCE VICKERY, HOLISTIC PHYSICIAN.

Some revered Vince Vickery as the greatest healer in all of Tennessee. Others dismissed the man as a quack. The facts were these: Over the course of his medical career, Vince had predicted, with complete accuracy, the fate of every one of his patients—whether they would die or live. And for those patients bound to live, Vince had cured them of their ailments with nothing more than a homemade herbal broth. He had carried on this practice for more than thirteen years.

The townspeople could wonder and speculate, but Felix knew it was Death who granted his father such powers. His father was contractually bound to Death as an apprentice, and on Felix's sixteenth birthday, he too would be offered a lifelong apprenticeship.

No one in town knew Felix Vickery existed. He was forbidden to enter Boone Ridge and instead required to stay in the wood, near Poplar House, where he served as apprentice-in-training every day of the year.

Every day save this one, Halloween, when Death took a vacation.

One day out of every year, the Death of Boone Ridge claimed no lives. He packed a carpetbag and left Poplar House at dawn, and he did not return until dawn of the next day. Felix did not ask *where* it was that Death went—that didn't matter. What mattered was that everything changed on Halloween. On this one day, the house turned warm, no patients came to visit, and those at death's door continued to live and breathe. On this day, Felix was permitted to leave Poplar Wood.

"What're you doing, still working away?"

Felix looked up from the stove, where he had been busily bent over a broth of rose petals and nightshade. This was his father's most popular concoction—a remedy that alleviated bad bouts of the flu.

"I thought I'd brew some reserve," said Felix. "It's the season, after all."

Vince smiled at his son. He was not an old man, but he had an old smile, his lips strained from waking too many mornings under hoary frost. Still, to Felix, on this day, that smile was the most welcome sight in all the world. It meant *freedom*.

"Leave the broth to cool," Vince told his son, "and be off with you."

Carefully, Felix removed the pot from the stove and placed it on the waiting trivet. Then he obeyed his father's second command with more relish, grabbing his satchel and bursting out of the house, onto the front porch.

The day that had been leaking in now dunked Felix in its amber light. At the top of the hill facing Poplar House, the light splashed on something particularly amber. It was a pile of hair, and it belonged to Felix's twin brother.

Felix raised a hand to block the sun from his seeing eye—the one not murky white and covered with an eyepatch. At the hill's crest, backed by the setting sun, Lee Vickery looked like a king.

"Happy Halloween!" Lee bellowed. He set off down the hill, his lanky legs propelling him toward the house at an alarming speed.

"Happy Halloween!" Felix called back.

Lee catapulted onto the porch and slung his brother into his arms, laughing. They teetered, then tottered, and before Felix could extract himself, they crashed to the floor.

Once they had righted themselves, Lee smacked Felix's sneaker. "You ready?"

Felix raised his satchel.

"Excellent," said Lee. "I'll be out in three minutes. Time me."

Felix noted the second hand of his wristwatch as Lee clattered into the west end of Poplar House. Above that door was a plaque that read JUDITH VICKERY, PSYCHIATRIST. The door hinges moaned as the wind coaxed out the smell of basil and sharp cheese. The boys' mother was cooking.

Felix's stomach turned over, pleased but agonized. He wondered if his mother hummed while she cooked. He bet she did. He bet it was the most beautiful sound in the world—better even than the cheery lull of crickets.

Lee toppled out wearing a heavier jacket.

"I will, I will!" he called into the house.

Felix checked the second hand. "Two minutes, twenty seconds."

Lee grinned, victorious. He handed Felix a warm cheddar biscuit, and the boys set out for town.

"Mom said to be home at eleven," Lee pouted.

"That's later than last year."

"Yeah, but not as long as Dad lets you stay out."

"Not as long as I *could* stay out," said Felix. "But I'll walk home with you. Like always."

Lee kicked a branch, then looked at Felix, watching him closely with clear brown eyes.

"I keep thinking that one year you'll . . . well, you'll want to stay out on your own. It *is* your only chance to see town. If I could stay out . . ." He said nothing more, but Felix could guess his brother's thoughts: curious wonderings of what lay beyond curfew.

"I don't like town," Felix said. "Too much happens there, too quickly."

"That's *why* I like it." Lee laughed.

Unlike Felix, Lee often laughed. His west-end bedroom was separated from Felix's east-end room only by a mere two walls. Lee's laughter would sometimes bleed through the wood, and Felix would wonder what had caused the laugh—perhaps a joke their mother had made. Lee had told Felix that their mother made terrific jokes, but Felix had no way of knowing; he had never met their mother, just as Lee had never met their father. That was part of the Agreement.

"Tonight," Lee said, "I'm going to take you to Creek Diner. That's where everybody at school hangs out now. Then we'll go to the bonfire. And maybe you'll even talk to someone this year!"

Felix humphed and chewed his biscuit. He didn't go into town to talk to people. He went into town to *watch* and, most importantly, *learn*.

"Why aren't we dressing up?" Felix asked.

In the past, Lee had insisted on the two of them donning costumes before they went into Boone Ridge. Felix had always dressed as an explorer, which didn't require much beyond his father's wide-brimmed hat.

But Lee had told him a few days earlier that this year they would go in normal attire.

Lee shrugged. "People just don't dress up anymore."

"People?"

"Guys our age. Dressing up is for kids."

"Oh."

This was one of many things Felix would've known if he'd gone to Boone Ridge Middle School. He ached for the knowledge Lee collected and brought home each day. Perhaps, Felix thought, once he knew what other people did, he would want to talk to them.

But until then, he was grateful, at least, to not be burdened with all the rules Lee learned and followed at school: no gum-chewing, no playing tag after you turned ten, no acting like you knew all the answers in class. . . . And now, no costumes for Halloween.

Felix wondered if there was a way to learn all the world's great lessons—the history of ancient civilizations and the science of the stars—without having to learn all its exhausting rules, as well.

He wondered if one day he might get the chance to find out.

2
GRETCHEN

"EARTH TO EARTH, ashes to ashes, dust to dust."

They were pretty words, and the priest recited them like poetry, but Gretchen thought it was a terrible way to say goodbye. Essie Hasting's mother was crying, as were a dozen other people dressed in black. It had misted earlier that day, and wet grass clung to Gretchen's dress shoes. She watched Ms. Hasting, Essie's only family, throw a handful of damp dirt onto the lacquered coffin.

Essie's only family was crying, but none of Gretchen's family was. They were no friends of the Hastings—societal obligation had demanded their presence. Gretchen's father was the mayor of Boone Ridge, and Essie's death had been the town's greatest tragedy in recent years. *An unthinkable accident, a terrible loss*—that is what the townspeople called it. Essie Hasting, star student and captain of the Boone Ridge High dance team, had taken a walk on Monday night in Hickory Park, and there slipped on loose rocks and fallen into a ravine. The fall was from such a great height, the police reported, that Essie certainly died on impact.

An unthinkable accident.

That was *all* people said. As though there was nothing else to know about Essie's untimely demise. Gretchen, however, had questions:

Why had Essie Hasting been walking alone at night?

How could someone so young as Essie simply *die*?

And why had Mayor Whipple insisted on talking to the Boone Ridge sheriff and coroner behind shut office doors?

Gretchen might ask her questions aloud, but no one would tell her a thing. Not at home, because she was the baby of the family, and no one takes the baby seriously. And not in town, because she was the mayor's daughter, and people stitched their lips for fear that Gretchen would go blabbering their secrets to her powerful father.

So if Gretchen wanted answers, she would have to find them out on her own.

"Stop that, child."

Gram Whipple gripped bony fingers into Gretchen's shoulder, and Gretchen realized too late that she had been twirling her hair.

"Show some decorum," the old woman said, staring ahead at the burial plot.

Decorum—that was what this day was about. Duty and propriety, the great tenets of the Whipple household, even here, at the funeral of a family enemy. Gretchen clasped her hands behind her back, to keep them out of further trouble. She showed her best decorum as the last of the dirt fell upon Essie's coffin and the black-clad crowd began to disperse.

Essie's mother stood close to the grave, as friends gathered to console her. Two men with shovels were piling earth into the six-foot hole—a careless motion, like how Gretchen's father scooped sugar into his coffee. Gram and Mayor Whipple had broken away to speak to the priest, making a *decorous* show of concern for all the townspeople to see. Soon their work here would be done.

Beside her, Gretchen's brother, Asa, laughed.

"Stupid," he said. "This whole thing is stupid."

Asa was wearing a black suit, per Gram Whipple's orders, but a bright purple flower peeked from its breast pocket—loud and irreverent, decidedly wrong for a solemn occasion. There was a thick gauze bandage wound about his right palm, no doubt the result of some recent fight. Asa was always fighting.

People often told Gretchen she looked like Asa, and this frightened her. She had the same inky black hair and dark eyes, that much was true. Family friends also noted that both brother and sister had unusually red lips—the kind of red that normal people only achieve with the help of lipstick. But there, Gretchen hoped, the similarities ended, because Asa made the most awful faces. He smiled when there was nothing to be happy about, he sneered when he should've cried, and he flattened his mouth in distaste when others around him laughed. It was as though the muscles in Asa's face had been woven all wrong.

Now Gretchen gave him a sour look.

"Funerals aren't stupid," she told him. "What happened to Essie was awful, even if she was who she was. I'm showing decorum, and so should you."

A muscle twitched wrongly in Asa's jaw. "Like decorum changes anything. She's still dead, isn't she?"

Gretchen did not reply. She was looking beyond Asa, toward the border of Poplar Wood. At the top of a hill, two figures were standing among the trees, looking down on the cemetery. They had obviously not been invited to this burial.

"Hey!" she called out. "Hey! What do you think you're doing?"

Gretchen began to stomp up the hill, and as she moved up, she got a better look at the intruders. One was tall and russet-haired, with lanky limbs; Gretchen recognized him from school. The other boy was short and small, and his hair was just as dark as hers. Over one of his eyes, he wore a patch. At first, both boys looked down at Gretchen in bewilderment as though they thought she was talking to the poplars and not to them. Then realization touched the face of the one with the covered eye. He grabbed the elbow of the other, and the two boys fled back into the wood.

"Hey!" Gretchen called again. "What're you snooping around here for? Explain yourselves! I know who you are, LEE VICKERY!"

But Lee Vickery and his friend did not slow down, and Gretchen was left staring after them, new mud stains on her tights. She looked down the hill, to where Essie's mother was crying and Asa was kicking at sod. What was there for any snooper to see? Only drawn faces and mist and gloom—decorum at its worst. An end to an unthinkable accident, that was all.

Still, one question hung over Gretchen, like the low, damp clouds above:

Couldn't she dare to think the unthinkable?

3
LEE

THERE WERE MANY things about his twin brother that Lee Vickery did not understand. One was how Felix could be so content to talk to no one but Lee, their father, and Death. Another was why Felix did not like town. If Lee had been bound to work all his days within Poplar Wood until his sixteenth birthday, he would be itching to get away. He would've stayed out long past eleven o'clock on Halloween and into the dewy hours of dawn, to the very last seconds before Death returned from vacation.

Luckily, Lee wasn't bound to Poplar Wood. He could go to school and the grocery store and Creek Diner. He knew street names and kids his own age. Town was familiar, and every year he took pride in showing it off to Felix—the shops that had opened in the past year, the shops that had closed and shuttered their windows, the new streetlights and better-paved roads—as though he'd personally had a hand in paving the roads and laying the bricks of the stores.

The brothers walked down Main Street together, past storefronts decorated with pumpkins and fake cobwebs. The sun was slipping behind the town hall spire, and younger children dressed as superheroes and royalty were already on the streets, toting pillowcases and plastic buckets. Now that they were in town and far from Boone Cemetery, Lee's heart had fallen into a steadier patter. The sight of Gretchen Whipple storming toward them had been downright petrifying, but if Felix hadn't grabbed Lee, he might have stayed and tried to explain himself. They hadn't been snooping, after all. It was just that the cemetery bordered Poplar Wood, and passing through it was the quickest way into town.

"That girl wasn't nice," Felix said as they turned onto Hickory Street, the busiest road in town.

"She thought we were trying to cause trouble, I guess."

Lee did not mention that the girl was Gretchen Whipple. Felix already didn't like town, and running into one of the Whipples—the Vickeries sworn enemies—would hardly improve his opinion.

"Whose funeral was it?" Felix asked.

"Essie Hasting's."

This was a name Lee had not known until two days ago, when school had suddenly rippled with whispers about Essie, whose body had been found by hikers early that morning at the bottom of a steep cliff in Hickory Park. Lee didn't understand why everyone liked to whisper about it so much, like it was something exciting. Lee just felt sad about the whole thing.

"You and Dad wouldn't have seen her as a patient," he told Felix. "She died by accident."

"I wondered," Felix said softly. "A candle went out this week, but it wasn't someone Dad had attended to. Why didn't you tell me?"

Most days, when Lee came home from school, he told Felix all about what was going on in town, whether Felix wanted to hear or not.

"Dunno." Lee shrugged. "Guess it slipped my mind."

But the truth was that Lee hadn't told Felix on purpose. There was already so much talk of death and *Death* at Poplar House, and Lee got tired of it.

"Here we are!"

They had arrived at Creek Diner. The diner wasn't situated anywhere near a creek, but rather on a street called Creek Lane. It was a small brick building with extra-large windows, booth seats, and a soda fountain. In the corner of the restaurant, a group of boys with close-cropped hair sat drinking sodas and sharing a big plate of fries. They looked to be around Lee's age, but he told Felix, "I don't know those guys."

"Good," said Felix. "I don't want to meet anyone."

They sat down at the counter, and Mr. Harvey, a potbellied man with a goatee, came to take their order. Lee studied the chalkboard specials and then ordered a salted caramel shake and a plate of fried pickles for the both of them.

"That's expensive," Felix said, once Mr. Harvey had gone back to the kitchen.

"Yeah. Mom gave me some money."

Lee pulled a tattered wallet out of his back pocket. Vince may have given Felix a later curfew, but Judith gave Lee a better allowance.

The store bell clanged, and Lee turned too quick to realize he shouldn't have turned at all.

"What're you looking at, carrot top?"

Asa Whipple had walked into Creek Diner. He strode straight over and flicked Lee's ear.

"Teach you to gawk," he said, hurtling over the counter and barging into the kitchen, shouting, "Clocking in, Mr. Harvey!"

"Since when did he start working here?" Lee muttered.

22

"Your ear's red," said Felix. "Why'd you let him do that?"

Lee touched his throbbing ear. "It's Asa. That's just what you gotta do."

"Asa *Whipple*?"

So much for keeping up Felix's opinion of town. It seemed the brothers were fated to run into every Whipple in existence.

Lee had told Felix all about Asa. He was a junior at Boone Ridge High and was feared far and wide by every kid in town. He was strong and fast, and he enjoyed picking on anyone even an inch shorter than him. He beat up plenty of people just for looking at him funny. He'd been suspended from school four times but never expelled because he was the mayor's son. And since he'd turned sixteen and gotten a motorbike, he'd been able to terrorize the town's younger citizens all the more conveniently.

Mr. Harvey emerged from the back with an iced glass mug of caramel shake and a piping-hot plate of fried pickles, which made Lee forget all about his stinging ear.

"You're going to love these." Lee waved a pickle under Felix's nose. "I bet Dad doesn't make anything as good as fried pickles."

"We've been eating a lot of bean soup lately," said Felix, cutting at a pickle with his knife and fork.

Lee laughed and grabbed the knife from Felix's hand. "Not like that. Like this."

He dangled a whole pickle spear above his mouth and chomped down half of it. Green juice ran out the corner of his mouth.

Felix took his knife back and continued to saw his food. "This is the way we do things in my part of the house."

"Fine," Lee said, resigned and wondering just how many things about Poplar House's east end he would never find out.

And all because of the stupid Agreement. Had the Agreement not existed, there would be no east or west ends at all. Lee took a long gulp of caramel shake, only to contract a terrible case of brain freeze.

"*Oww*," he yowled, thudding his head on the counter.

"We drink our drinks slower, too," Felix said, smiling a little.

Lee lifted his head. "Thanks a lot." Rubbing at his temples, he said, "Do you ever think maybe we just did it wrong?"

It had been almost two years since the brothers had tried out their plan—a plan to break the Agreement once and for all. They had failed, and they had been punished and warned to never try again. Human plots were nothing against the will of the Shades, especially plots crafted by humans as young and weak as Lee and Felix. That is what Death had told them. Lee's left ear could still hear every word carried on the dark, oily voice of his brother's master.

The Agreement was permanent, and not a thing to be broken. The terms were these:

Poplar House would forever be divided into two parts— EAST *and* WEST.

On the east side, Felix would live
with his father and Death.

On the west side, Lee would live with
his mother and Memory.

Their parents would never set eyes on each
other for the rest of their days.

Felix would never see his mother, and
Lee would never see his father.

The twins could meet, but only
outside the house.

That was the Agreement, and it would stand in perpetuity. The brothers had learned this the hard way. But every so often Lee let himself wonder if there was another way—a way to break the Agreement that the brothers hadn't yet tried.

"You shouldn't get your hopes up," Felix said. "Those are the patients we have the most trouble with— the ones who hope when they shouldn't."

Lee chewed on his pickle. "You should *always* hope. That's what Mom says."

"That's because Mom lives with Memory, and Memory's kinder. But even if Memory would allow us all to see each other again, Death wouldn't. He never changes his mind."

"I wish we lived in another town," Lee said. "I hear the Death in Chattanooga is nice. His apprentice gives out chocolate candies so you have a sweet journey to the afterlife."

Felix scoffed. "I don't see how sugar makes the dying any better."

Lee noticed that Mr. Harvey had stopped cleaning the counter. He was standing still, staring at the brothers. Felix might not have known it, but Lee did: Ordinary people looked at you funny when you talked about Death and Memory as though they were real people who made Agreements.

"Come on," Lee said, placing a wad of money on the counter. "Let's go."

"But we're not done."

Lee took the last two fried pickles, wrapped them in a napkin, and shoved them into his coat pocket. "Now we are. We want a good spot for the bonfire."

Felix sighed but followed Lee out of the diner. Lee looked back only once, through the glass of the closed door. Mr. Harvey was no longer watching them, but someone else was. Asa smiled a horrible smile in Lee's direction. He raised two fingers to his eyes, then pointed them at Lee. A gesture to say *I'm watching you, kid.*

Lee shuddered. He had a sneaking suspicion that even if the Whipples and Vickeries weren't sworn enemies, Asa Whipple still wouldn't be his friend.

4
FELIX

NIGHT WAS THICK over Main Street. The streetlights had not turned on as they ought to have, and corners Felix thought he knew from Halloweens past were darkened, all unfamiliar.

"Why aren't the lights working?" he asked.

"It's because of that storm," said Lee. "A big bolt of lightning knocked out something electrical, and they haven't been able to fix it yet. It's . . . a little creepy."

"Right time for it, though, I guess."

"Oh, definitely," Lee said, even as he shivered.

A light appeared in the distance. It came from Featherstone Park, where the Halloween bonfire was held each year. As they walked toward it, Felix wrapped an arm around his brother. He wasn't going to tease Lee for being a little creeped out. If Felix hadn't lived with Death his whole life, he knew he'd be scared, too. Felix understood very well why kids his age were afraid of dark streets. He understood why tales of werewolves and bloodied maniacs sent gooseflesh tickling up the skin. He *understood* those fears very well—but he never *felt* them.

It wasn't that Felix considered himself braver than his brother or other boys his age. He just didn't fear ghosts, blood, and darkness, because he knew what he *did* need to fear: Death, the Shade he served. It was a fear so great and constant that Felix wondered if it had simply pushed out all the normal fears to make room for itself and itself alone.

"Watch it, would you?"

Felix had been so lost in his thoughts he hadn't noticed a girl's sparkly shoe underfoot.

"Sorry, it's hard to see," said Lee, tugging Felix away from the girl, who was dressed like an angel and scowling so hard through her glittery makeup that even her tinsel halo seemed provoked. The bonfire light was bright here, and Felix could see just fine, but the girl had been on his unseeing side.

"Come on," Lee said to Felix. "We've got to find our friend."

"Find our friend" was Lee's way of fibbing their way to the front of the crowd. It meant crawling underneath arms and through legs and just barely avoiding elbows in the face. When it was all over, the boys were so close to the fire that Felix's seeing eye stung with smoke.

The bonfire swelled before them, a great big arrogant thing. Sparks cracked out, whizzing into the night. Beside Felix, a grown woman chomped greedily at a candy apple; it was a gruesome sight, all red shards and unchecked spit. Felix closed his eye and took a deep breath, inhaling the smell of burning wood and frost-nipped leaves. Around him, people spoke—dozens of voices all ducking and weaseling in and around each other. The sound of conversation was still strange to Felix, no matter how many Halloweens he had heard it.

"You!"

Felix opened his eye to find a nose at his chin. It was a particular nose, pinched at the bridge and rounded at the end like a jelly bean. Felix backed away from a girl with wild black hair, which was matted so badly it looked like it belonged to a poorly treated stuffed animal. Fake blood leaked from her mouth, and purple crescents puffed beneath her eyes. It was the eyes that Felix recognized: This was the girl from earlier, at the cemetery. Though the rest of her looked like an undead monster, her eyes were very much alive with anger, and they were fixed on Lee.

"What was that about?" she demanded. "Why were the two of you funeral crashing?"

Lee opened his mouth to the approximate circumference of a soup bowl. No sound came out.

"Just what's so interesting about a burial, huh? Don't you know it's not polite to stare while dead people are getting shoved in the ground? Don't you know it's rude to stare, period? What, Lee Vickery, have you lost the capacity for speech?"

Lee closed up his mouth. It looked as though he'd forgotten what words were. There was no choice, Felix decided. He would have to be the one to speak.

"We didn't know there was a funeral going on," he said. "We were just walking into town, and you don't own the cemetery, so leave us alone."

This was why Felix hated talking to people. They didn't understand anything, and they assumed and they yelled and they pointed fingers, just as the girl was doing now. Her pointing finger was so close to his face, he swatted it away.

"How dare you!" she cried, though she now looked more excited than angry. "Who is this, Lee? I've never seen him around." She turned to Felix. "You don't go to school with us, do you?"

Felix shook his head.

"Then you go to Harpeth Prep?"

Felix shook his head again.

"So you're from out of town."

Felix considered this. "Yes."

The girl squinted. "What's your name?"

Felix didn't answer, so the girl said, "My name's Gretchen."

"That's nice."

Gretchen frowned. "Fine. If you won't tell me your name, I'll just call you . . . *Zeke*. You've got a lot of nerve, hitting a girl like that, Zeke."

"I didn't hit you! Have you ever heard of personal sp—"

"Inconsequential." Gretchen turned to Lee and looked him over from toe to brow. "Why aren't you wearing a costume? It's Halloween, doofus."

Lee looked sheepish. "Don't you think we're too old for costumes?"

"Everyone wears a costume on Halloween. Even this weird friend of yours is."

"No I'm not," said Felix.

"Sure you are. You're a pirate."

"No," said Felix, "I'm not."

"Cut the tomfoolery, Zeke! What do you call *this*?"

Gretchen grabbed at Felix's eyepatch. It bent under her thumb and hit Felix's forehead with a stinging smack. Gretchen stepped back. "Whoa. Oh, *whoa*. Is that real?"

Shame swam into Felix's cheeks and burned them, stovetop hot. He didn't answer Gretchen. He ran. He thudded into the chest of a clown, then spun out and knocked a glass of cider from a princess's hand. He didn't apologize. He pressed on, beating through flesh and fabric until he was past the crowd entirely. Even then, he kept running, until he stumbled over a branch and fell right into Poplar Wood.

He sat up, heart a-thump, plucking out sprigs of pine needles that had lodged into his shoes.

"Felix? Felix!"

Lee emerged, panting, and hurried to kneel beside Felix, who shrank away.

"Don't touch me, I'm fine."

"She didn't know," Lee said, breathless. "Really, she didn't, Felix, or—"

"Doesn't matter." Felix got to his feet. "I told you I don't like town, and I don't like the people here. Now do you finally get why?"

"But that's just the way people are sometimes! Strangers. People who don't know you like I do."

"I saw how she looked at me," Felix said. "I'm going back home. Now."

"Please don't—"

"You don't have to come with me!" he snapped.

"Hey!" someone else cried.

Gretchen was standing at the wood's edge, looking very much like the zombie she'd dressed up as—shoulders hunched and bloodied mouth agape.

"Wait!" she said, but Felix darted into the dark of the wood.

It wasn't until a stitch twisted into his side that he slowed and stooped and puffed out stammers of breath, pressing his hand against an oak tree to keep himself upright.

Lee came up behind him once more. "You're not going back to the bonfire, are you?" he asked.

"No. I'm going home."

"But you're taking the long way back."

"I don't care."

Lee sighed loudly. "Fine. You were gonna walk back early with me; I'll walk back early with you. But Felix?"

"Yeah."

"I think you're being stupid."

"Okay."

That settled, the brothers started back toward Poplar House, leaving behind the bonfire and the girl named Gretchen.

In all his talks about town, Lee had only ever mentioned one person named Gretchen, and never in nice terms. Which could only mean that that undead girl had to be Gretchen *Whipple*. Felix reflected, with a grim smile, on what Halloween luck that was: His one night in town, and he had managed to run into *two* sworn enemies.

5

GRETCHEN

GRETCHEN WAS IN the counselor's office for the third time that week, and it was only Tuesday.

"Do you know why you're here?"

Ms. Clark, Boone Ridge Middle's school counselor, sat across from Gretchen at a snot-yellow desk. Her hands were folded neatly atop Gretchen's file, a manila folder as thick as a phone book.

"Guess you're going to tell me," Gretchen said.

Ms. Clark pulled in a short, forbearing breath. "You're here, Gretchen, because I want to help you. I want you to succeed in your classes. I want you to *learn.*"

Gretchen sat up straight. She folded her hands on the edge of the desk, a perfect mirror of Ms. Clark—

only Gretchen's nails were painted orange, and there was a ring drawn around her pinky finger in permanent marker.

"I want to learn, too," she said. "Mr. Edmonson is getting in the way."

Mr. Edmonson was Gretchen's history teacher, and according to the message Gretchen had left on his whiteboard that afternoon, he wasn't doing a very good job.

Ms. Clark showed Gretchen her cell phone screen. There was a photograph of Gretchen's handiwork, which had since been erased by an incensed Mr. Edmonson. The message was a poem:

> *Feed us knowledge, not facts.*
> *Give us hearts, not spineless backs.*
> *Don't test us on our As and Bs.*
> *Let us argue, read, and breathe.*

"It's got a nice rhythm," said Gretchen. "My best poem to date."

Ms. Clark clicked off her phone. "This is not poetry class, Gretchen. And that wasn't a poem, it was juvenile behavior. Do you know what 'juvenile' means?"

"'Juvenile.' Adjective. From the Latin *juvenilis*. There are several definitions, but I'm guessing the one you intended is 'childish, immature.'"

Ms. Clark slammed down her phone. Gretchen wasn't scared. She was used to making adults angry.

"Miss Whipple, I hope you don't find this funny."

"I don't," said Gretchen. "It's extremely serious. But haven't I given you the right answer? You can't be angry with me for that. Rights and wrongs and trues and falses—that's what you people want."

"'We people'? Who, pray tell, are 'we people'?"

"You, Mr. Edmonson, the principal. You just want us to color the right bubbles on our tests. None of you wants us to think, to wonder *what if*, because if we did that, we might get an answer wrong." Gretchen paused, but Ms. Clark didn't deny a thing. "Only Mr. Hickering asks us whys. Yesterday, Quentin Mattherson finished this really difficult long division on the board. Quentin is the teachers' favorite, obviously, because he always gives the right answers.

"But then, do you know what Mr. Hickering said? He asked Quentin *why* what he'd done was so important. 'Why does division matter, Quentin?' he asked. 'It's all fine and good you understand decimal points, but why on earth should any of us care?'"

Gretchen leaned in closer. "And Quentin didn't know any right answer to that. He told Mr. Edmonson, 'I just want an A.' Isn't that the stupidest thing you've ever heard? Quentin didn't know why he should care, and he didn't care that he didn't."

"There is nothing wrong with wanting As," said Ms. Clark. "Good students want to make good grades. And you have the potential to do just that, if only you didn't argue so much."

"But arguing is how we learn," said Gretchen. "That's what Dad always says."

"Well, please do remind your father of that when you give him this." Ms. Clark handed Gretchen a sinister green slip of paper.

"Fine!" Gretchen chirped brightly.

"You understand, don't you, Miss Whipple, that you are one demerit away from a suspension?"

"Of course," said Gretchen. "Why do you think I'm smiling?"

Gretchen stepped outside Boone Ridge Middle just as Asa was pulling Whipplesnapper into the parking lot. Whipplesnapper was a car the color of green mold, and it smelled even worse. The family was rich enough for Asa to afford not only his motorbike, but a brand-new sports car. Mayor Whipple had even taken his son to many car lots, attempting to convince Asa to buy a nice BMW.

Only, Asa did not want a nice BMW. He wanted Whipplesnapper, a car that was older than Gretchen, which he'd bought from a used car lot in Junction City, twenty miles east of Boone Ridge. As for his motorbike—he'd bought that broken and brought it to life himself. For weeks, the Whipples' driveway had been oil-stained and covered in chrome parts. Gram had made a fuss, but for those few weeks, Asa had almost seemed happy. Almost. And then he'd cleared the mess away and gone back to his all-wrong smiles.

"You're late," Gretchen told Asa, settling into the passenger seat.

"*You're* late," Asa grunted back.

"I had a special appointment."

Asa shifted Whipplesnapper's gears. The old sedan wheezed out of the parking lot and clunked onto the main road. As they drove away from school, Gretchen stuck her head out the window and proudly surveyed the chalk message on the brick overhang—the reason for her first counselor visit that week.

QUESTION EVERYTHING, it read.

Asa was looking at his rearview mirror, and Gretchen was sure he could see her chalky masterpiece. She wondered if he approved—not that she wanted *Asa's* approval, and not that he'd ever tell her if she had it.

"They kicking you out, or what?" he asked.

"I'm one demerit away from suspension," Gretchen said breezily.

Asa snorted. Her older brother had his own impressive suspension record, Gretchen knew, though his was for fights and cigarettes, not protest poems. But maybe Asa's snort meant he was proud of her. Not that she cared. She really didn't, at all.

Asa slowed the car at a red light. "Just because you don't hand in those slips to Gram or Dad doesn't mean they don't know about your demerits. I've heard them talking about sending you off."

Gretchen laughed, but it was a puttery sound, much like Whipplesnapper's engine. "You're making that up. Send me off to where?"

"North Carolina. I'm sure Gram's picked the school with the ugliest uniforms and worst food. Someplace with lots of *decorum*." Asa simpered at Gretchen, and she dropped her eyes to her shoes.

"The light's green," she muttered.

"You keep acting out at this rate, they'll ship you off by New Year's."

"The light's green!" Gretchen yelled.

Asa laughed and turned back to the road. Whipplesnapper shuddered through the intersection.

Asa was lying, he had to be. Gram wouldn't send Gretchen away to boarding school. She hadn't sent Asa away, for all his black eyes and green slips. But then, Asa had always gotten away with more. He was the firstborn, the only son. He was the one who'd inherit the family business. And Gretchen? Maybe she was only good for sending away.

"Whatever," said Gretchen. "'Act out' is a very stupid pairing of verb and preposition. Practically redundant. Acting, by its very definition, is an outward activity."

Whipplesnapper rumbled down Main Street and turned onto Avenue B, then rattled to a stop in front of the Whipples' well-manicured lawn. Cherubic statues watched them, arrows drawn and aimed for fatal blows. Bushes lined the house, cut into perfect squares. The whole of the lawn seemed to take offense at Whipplesnapper's wheezing presence.

Asa cut the engine, and the ruckus stopped.

"You *do* question everything," Asa said.

Gretchen sniffed proudly. "You'd better believe it."

"Good."

Gretchen frowned. "*Good?*" That almost sounded like a compliment.

"You go right ahead questioning. You question yourself right over the Smoky Mountains. I've always wanted a second bedroom." Grinning, Asa got out of the car and strode across the front lawn, leaving a trodden path through the tender grass.

Stupid, Gretchen thought. *Stupid to ever think Asa would say something nice.* He wanted Gretchen around as much as Gram and her father did—not at all. And really, what was she good for at home? Asa was the one who'd been trained in the ways of summoning, and she would never be. So what was the point of being a secondborn Whipple? All she could do was stand outside the family business she'd never be a part of.

So maybe, Gretchen reflected, it would be better to be sent away to school. In North Carolina, she might meet teachers who encouraged independent thought. She might even make friends—kids her age who didn't care what her last name was. That might be worth the ugly uniforms and the subpar food.

Only, North Carolina didn't have the answers Gretchen needed right now. Her questions had to do with a park in Boone Ridge and a conversation she had heard right here in her own home.

The day the hikers had found Essie's body, Gretchen had listened on the other side of her father's office wall, using the drinking glass that, over many years of eavesdropping, she'd determined was best for the job. In the office were Orson Moser, the Boone Ridge sheriff, and Vernon Wilkes, the town coroner.

"You're sure?" asked Mayor Whipple.

"Certain," said the coroner, his deep voice dulled

through the wall. "Her body was found in that ravine, but without one broken bone. Not a bruise, not a scratch—no discernable cause of death."

"And yet," said Sheriff Moser, "the girl is dead."

"The hikers," said Mayor Whipple. "Do they know anything?"

"Young kids," said the sheriff. "Called us first thing, not one of 'em touched the body. Clear as day when they found her that she was gone."

"Good," said Mayor Whipple. "Then our story will stand."

"And what story is that?" asked the coroner.

"That she fell from the cliff, of course. Loose rocks, slippery from the storm. She lost her footing and tragically fell to her death."

"Whipple," said Sheriff Moser. "This warrants investigation."

"Hardly," said Mayor Whipple. "I know who the culprit is."

"Who?" asked the joined voices of coroner and sheriff.

"Death," said Mayor Whipple. "It was Death who killed the girl. He took her, before her appointed time, for reasons of his own."

"But!" cried Sheriff Moser. "Surely that's out of line with—"

"Your job, gentlemen, is to do as your mayor asks. Essie Hasting's death was a tragic accident. She fell from a cliff in Hickory Park, down to the rocks below. The town will mourn her, and my family will pay our respects. Then, this town will move on."

The silence was so long and complete Gretchen feared she'd missed something, and she pressed her ear more firmly to her listening glass.

"That," said Sheriff Moser, "is what you'd like us to say?"

"That is what *happened*," said Mayor Whipple. "We are all agreed: *That is what happened that night.*"

"Of course," said the coroner, in his deep drawl. "My report will confirm that."

Gretchen had run to her room then, ears burning from the words still circling inside them:

Culprit.

Investigation.

Not a bruise, not a scratch.

Even now, Gretchen felt dirty, as though those words needed to be washed clean from her ears with a cotton swab.

Death had killed Essie Hasting.

Death killed everyone, of course. Gretchen knew that. But the way her father and the two men spoke made it sound like this was different. Like this was wrong. Only they would tell no one about it. They would keep it quiet.

Something was not right.

Something was hidden.

And her father was hiding it.

Maybe Gretchen wasn't the firstborn Whipple, wasn't destined to be a summoner. But just because she was shut out of the family business didn't mean she couldn't try to break in.

Her father was hiding a secret, and Gretchen was going to uncover it.

She'd prove that she was just as much a Whipple as the rest of them.

So, for now, she had to stay in Boone Ridge. North Carolina would have to wait. And if that required fewer poems and demerits—well, she could manage that.

Resolved, Gretchen crumpled the green slip of paper, and headed inside.

6

LEE

LEE TIED A violet bow around the canning jar. Violet-ribboned jars belonged on the fifth shelf, which Lee wasn't yet tall enough to reach without the stepladder. Judith was in the parlor, still talking with Mrs. Derry, her five o'clock appointment. When Lee entered the room, he looked neither woman in the eye, only took the splintery stepladder, which his mother had left propped by the china cabinet, and lugged it to the canning room so he could properly put away Mrs. Derry's memory.

It must have been a terrible one, Lee thought, running his thumb along the puckered rim of the jar. Its contents were black as night, thick as syrup. Still fresh, the memory bubbled and squelched. It had to be atrocious. That was why it belonged on the fifth shelf.

The stepladder squeaked under Lee's foot. He reached high and nudged the jar into its place, making sure its label—*Forget*—was visible. Then he climbed down, wound up the rest of the ribbon, and put it away with the sewing scissors. That was that—a chore complete.

Before Lee reached for the light switch, he stopped and stared at the wall of jars. He couldn't help it; it was as natural an instinct as scratching an itch. Those five shelves of memories were a sight to behold.

The first and lowest shelf was the fullest, crammed with silver-filled jars of Trivialities—accidents and mishaps and misspoken words, tied neatly at their tops with blue ribbon. On the second shelf, the orange-ribboned jars were filled to their brims with what an uninformed visitor would swear to be lemonade. These were memories of People, down to the timbre of a laugh and the shade of a freckle. Green-ribboned jars of clear Happiness rested on the fourth shelf. The dark, violet-ribboned memories of Bad Things, like Mrs. Derry's, were above them on the fifth. But the memories Lee found most entrancing sat on the third shelf. They were red-ribboned memories of Love, the exact shade and substance of cherry cordial, and they simmered in their jars, as though each was suspended over a flame.

Then there was the matter of labeling memories. Green-ribboned jars were universally marked *Remember.*

They were memories siphoned by his mother, stored here to be kept safe, untainted by time or disease. Memories worth reliving.

The blue- and violet-ribboned jars were nearly all labeled *Forget*. Memories his mother coaxed out, to ease the minds of their bearers, then sealed away to never be opened again. They were full of pain or sadness or embarrassment. Memories best put away.

But the memories of Love and of People—there was no rule to their labeling. They were equal parts *Remember* and *Forget*. Some precious, to be cherished. Some rotten, to be put away. And they were the only jars Lee was ever asked to relabel. Patients would return, begging to never remember former friends whose memories they once wished to preserve, while others asked to reclaim memories of love they once thought they did not want anymore.

Once jars marked *Forget* had sat untouched for a year, Lee took them down from their shelves and disposed of them for good. This was Lee's least favorite part of the job, for it required that he venture deep into Poplar Wood, to a small and clear pond. There, he slowly opened each of the jars under the water's surface and let the memories free.

There was magic in the place that Lee called Forgetful Pond. Memory had formed it long ago with her power—water that washed away memories for all time. Lee didn't like staying near the pond for any length of time. It spoke to him in dark and greedy whispers, and Lee had a notion that should he ever fall into the water, he would lose every memory inside his head and simply cease to exist. Whatever magic lived in the pond, Lee had decided, was not a nice kind of magic. He avoided trips whenever he could, setting aside the jars to be disposed of and only venturing out once or twice a year. His mother and Memory didn't seem to mind this. So long as the jars were promptly labeled and shelved from the beginning, all was well in the house's west end. Meantime, Memory kept the sole record of appointments—which patients had produced which memories, and how much of each. The practice was tidy and orderly, as Lee's work was expected to be.

His staring complete, Lee flicked off the light of the canning room and locked the door tight. Behind him, he heard a noise like a popping knuckle. He only heard that noise out of his left, otherwise-unhearing ear. It was Memory.

Memory was in the hallway, but she didn't speak to Lee. She only passed by, invisible as always, humming a tune that was deep and minor-keyed. The back screen door squeaked open, caught in the grasp of an unseasonably warm November wind. Then the door clattered against its frame, and the humming faded away.

Lee peered into the parlor. Mrs. Derry had left, and Judith sat alone in her wicker chair, looking at the jade and pearl bracelet around her wrist. Lee had heard the history of that bracelet more than a dozen times over, but he never tired of it.

As a young apprentice to Death, Lee's father had found the bracelet beneath a boulder at the base of Boone Falls, just at the point where the white water hit hardest. The bracelet had slipped from a crevice and landed perfectly in Vince Vickery's outstretched hand. He'd lost his balance immediately after and slipped into the water, conking his head on the rocky river base. His coat had snagged in a bramble bush overhanging the river, and it had been there that Judith Birdwhistle—young apprentice to Memory—found him, unconscious. She'd lugged him out on her own and pressed her lips to his, breathing air back into his lungs. Soon after Vince had revived, he gave his newfound bracelet—which he'd meant to pawn for winter supplies—to his rescuer, along with a promise of eternal devotion.

That day had been Halloween, when Death had been on vacation, and Memory, too, had been otherwise occupied. Neither Shade had been watching their apprentice, but the third Shade had: Passion. Thanks to Passion, Judith and Vince had fallen in love fierce and fast, before Death or Memory could prevent their rival apprentices from speaking. The other two Shades only had a say in things later—a say that became an Agreement.

"All done?" Lee asked his mother.

She started and looked up.

"Last patient of the day," she said.

"They were bad memories."

"Yes." Judith's face was off-color, as it often was after sessions. "You sealed them well?"

Lee had been handling jars since his tenth birthday, and Judith never failed to ask him this question. If a jar broke or its lid came loose, the contents would be set free. That memory would no longer belong to the patient who had surrendered it, but to whomever stood nearest the damage. Or, if no one was near, the memory would simply disappear, lost forever.

Even though he knew these risks, Lee had a habit of carelessness in the canning room. Many times before, he'd tied orange ribbons where green ones ought to have gone or shelved memories of People with the memories of Love, which resulted in patients returning to Judith to say how they felt a sudden affection for their grocer, without knowing why. Even worse, just last month, Lee hadn't properly sealed a memory of a Triviality, and it had evaporated overnight.

Memory had not been happy about that. Though she'd said nothing to Lee, he'd heard her arguing with his mother late into the night, and the next day, he'd heard Memory's moody humming at his ear as he sealed and stored a new set of jars. She'd kept close by him for weeks after that, to be sure he did his job correctly.

"Very well sealed," Lee reported. "I think I'll go out to the porch for a while."

"Supper in half an hour," his mother replied.

She knew that Lee went out to the porch to meet with Felix, the son she could never know. If Lee thought on this for long, it made him unspeakably sad. So he did not think about it tonight. He tromped out to the front porch and settled on its top step. There he stared into the dark of Poplar Wood, his hearing ear perked for the sound of Felix's footsteps.

1
FELIX

FELIX PLACED THE last of the white snakeroot inside his satchel. His knuckles were stiff from so much plucking and digging. Even so, Felix liked herb collecting on days like today. Here in the wood, he was far from the chill of the house and the sight of Death and the stench of the red candles burning in the cellar.

This was the last of the warm autumn days—Felix was sure of it. True November was about to arrive. That was why Felix had been hard at work all day, collecting each herb itemized on his father's list. Now, his satchel heavy and fat, Felix walked home, carrying with him a pungent mingle of smells.

A lit lantern shone from the west end of Poplar House. *Lee.* Felix could remember a not-too-distant time when his brother had waited on him with eager eyes and a book in hand. In those days, Lee had been so sure there was a way to break the Agreement. He'd checked out dozens of books from the Boone Ridge library, with titles like *Magic and Its Practicalities* and *The Art of Spell-Breaking.* Lee had been full of hope then, convinced he would soon hear his father's stories in the east end's parlor and that Felix would cook with his mother in the west end's kitchen. But that had been before. Before Felix had been thrown in the cellar and Lee was sent in the dead of night to Forgetful Pond, where he'd emptied memories until the break of day. Light punishments, Death and Memory had told them, for attempting to fool the Shades.

Felix drew nearer the porch, and at last Lee noticed and waved him closer. "Took you long enough! I thought the gloaming goblins had got you for sure."

"Ready to run?" Felix asked.

Their attempt to break the Agreement had mostly been Lee's idea. He had done the reading and dreaming and planning. When that was over—over for good—Lee had diverted his energies into something else: running. Lee would often run circles around the house, begging Felix to watch the clock and root him on toward his best time yet. Felix didn't mind, because Lee was happy when he ran, and Felix had worried for a while that Lee's smile might have disappeared forever.

"Don't feel much like running tonight," said Lee. "Just talking."

"Bad memories?" Felix asked, sitting beside him.

Lee sometimes got into a funk when he had canned too many Bad Things.

A silence wound around the boys, tight like thread pulled around a spool.

Quietly, Lee asked, "Do you think you could ever do it? Sign the contract?"

Felix shook his head. "Don't be stupid."

"So first I'm a coward, and now I'm stupid. I see how it is."

Lee returned his gaze to the trees, and Felix's heart sank to his stomach, sloshing around in acute discomfort. He wished he had never accused Lee of being a coward on Halloween night. He had meant to apologize, to tell Lee that he'd been upset, and the word had burst out like water from a weak dam. But he hadn't found the right way to say so.

"I didn't mean it that way," Felix said. "Of course I think about it, and I know Death does, too. He's already planning a way to trick me."

This was no idle worry in Felix's mind, but a fear born of reality: Both his parents had been tricked into their apprenticeships.

Felix knew their mother's story from Lee: Judith's mother had died in childbirth, and her father was all she had in the wide world. Matthias Birdwhistle had been Memory's apprentice before her, and he had been a kind man and a good father. He worked in an apothecary, where he snuck the town children toffees from the register jar, though he was supposed to charge a quarter. At the end of each day, he made up for the lost change from his own pocket.

Judith helped him with his work, tying ribbons and shelving memories the same as Lee did now. But Matthias had told Judith she could do far more than an apprenticeship would ever allow her. He wanted her to leave Boone Ridge and attend college, far away.

And Judith had meant to do just that. Until the day a bad man came to her father's shop, with a canvas bag in one hand and a pistol in the other. As Felix's grandfather picked up the phone to call the police, the bad man killed Matthias Birdwhistle, then and there, with a bullet.

That had been Judith's sixteenth birthday.

That day, Memory revealed herself to Judith, full of tender sympathy, and she made a deal: If Judith would sign her apprentice contract, Memory would take away all remembrance of her father's death.

So Judith signed, and even now she could not tell Lee a remembered detail of the robbery and murder. She only knew what she had read in the town newspaper about the crimes, nothing more. The worst of it was wiped clean, Judith's pain numbed from existence.

And then there was the boys' father. His family had long served Death. They had lived farther away from Boone Ridge proper, close to a coal mine where Vince's family worked. Mining was hard and unsafe, and Vince watched as his uncle and cousins came home late in the evening, faces darkened with soot, lungs filled with poison. But Vince's father was spared that fate, serving instead as Death's apprentice.

"As you will serve one day," Vince's father had told him. "You should be grateful for your higher calling."

But Vince had different ideas. When he turned sixteen, he was going to escape forever, hitchhiking up to Knoxville, or beyond. Only, when Vince turned sixteen, there was an accident at the mine, which crushed and suffocated men beneath the earth. That day, Vince begged Death to spare them—kind and good men with families to support.

"If you serve me," Death told him, "I can save their lives."

So Vince had signed his life away, and the line of Vickery apprentices continued.

Shades could not work without apprentices like Judith and Vince. Such helpers were hard to come by, and it only made sense that apprentices would train up their children to follow in their steps. And so apprentices' children were indentured until their sixteenth birthday. That was no Agreement, but standard practice. It meant far less work for everyone involved.

Only, Felix hated Death, and he hated his father's work and everything about Poplar House's east end. Felix did not mind about rarely seeing town or the people who lived there. But he did wish, dearly, that he could go to school. Though his father taught him reading and mathematics in the late afternoon, Felix envied the stories Lee brought back from Boone Ridge Middle: classes in science and even in painting and singing. A world of knowledge Felix would never know simply because Death kept him from it—simply because he was the less fortunate twin.

When he turned sixteen and Death handed him the contract to sign—that was when Felix would be free. He would refuse, rip the contract to shreds, and escape to a place where he could learn with no restrictions. He planned to go, go, *go* and never look back.

Only, he knew, his father had once made that very same plan.

And his father had not succeeded.

"We won't sign those contracts," Lee said now. "I sure hope we won't."

Hope. Lee used that word so often. How could he still hope *anything* after they'd tried their scheme and failed? Even if—*when*—they broke free from this house, the Agreement would remain in place.

So Felix would never be entirely free. Never free to see his mother, or hear her laughter, or tell her how much he loved her hot cheddar biscuits. Lee would never meet his father and memorize the lines of his face, take comfort in his kind smile. And Vince and Judith Vickery would never, ever meet again. No matter how much time passed, no matter what contracts were signed or unsigned—that Agreement remained in place.

Felix didn't hope. Still, he hated the Agreement. He hated it with a thick hatred that had pooled inside him since the day his father had sat him on his knee and told him the whole story of how he and Felix's mother had met.

A jade and pearl bracelet, caught in a riverbed. A misstep, a rescue, and a kiss. They had fallen in love that day, so fast and wholly. It was not until later that they discovered the small purple flowers tucked into their clothes and realized who the other was and, more importantly, who the other *belonged* to: a rival Shade.

Most towns' Shades lived with relative disinterest in each other's business. Death claimed lives and Memory remembrances and Passion fervent unions. They did what they pleased, on their own time. But in Boone Ridge, things were different. The Death and Memory of Boone Ridge despised each other with enduring ferocity. It was because of an argument they'd had years ago. Death had interfered in Memory's work, or perhaps it was Memory who had meddled in Death's— the details were murky now, so not even Felix's father knew them. What mattered was that the two Shades loathed one another, and a union between their apprentices was unthinkable. Impossible.

The Passion of Boone Ridge knew the depth of this hatred, and that was why Passion threw young Vince and Judith together that Halloween. For fun, to wreak havoc on two fellow Shades. So really, it was because of Passion that the Agreement existed, and though Felix had never met Passion, he hated that Shade as well. Hate made more sense than hope. But it was, Felix thought, more exhausting than hope, too.

Felix wondered at how quickly his good mood had soured. He no longer felt like talking to Lee for hours. His bones were suddenly weary from all his work.

"I'm tired," he said, clutching his satchel close. "It's been a long day."

"Oh. Okay."

These porch meetings, when Lee was through with school and Felix had finished the brunt of his chores—they were special. Only sometimes, they hurt too much. They reminded Felix of what could be, and what wasn't. They reminded him that they would never be a normal family that ate meals together and at night sat happily around a crackling fire. They were not a normal family in the slightest. They were just two brothers, one half-blind to all but Death and the other half-deaf to all but Memory, cursed to part ways at the end of each day.

Felix got to his feet. "I'll see you tomorrow, okay?"

"Yes. Okay."

Lee was still looking out to the wind-shaken wood.

Felix opened the east-end door and slammed it shut behind him. He crossed the kitchen without speaking to his father, who was stirring yet another herb broth on the stove. He stopped in the darkened doorway of the examination room. Here, Felix had watched Death remove fragile human lives with metal pincers as easily as Felix might discard a used tissue. He had seen the life flicker and fade from patients' eyes. He'd seen fear in those eyes, too, and a fight to push against the coming darkness until the last of their light was swallowed up. Every life had its appointed time—the moment its corresponding candle was set to extinguish forever, sending up curling blue smoke in the cellar. Felix had watched countless wicks sputter until no flame remained—lives gone, never to be relit. He had seen enough to know: You could not fight Death. So he did not know why the urge to do so remained thick and strong, knotted beneath his chest like a second heart.

He moved on down the hallway, slid shut the latch of his door, and lay upon his bed. It had begun to rain. Drops of water pelted against the house until a downpour sheeted his bedroom windows. Then Felix saw it, through his right eye, which could not see the rest of the world: a hand, pale and smooth, pressed against the window nearest his bed. The rainwater spewed around the fingers and into the empty flower box below. Felix stared harder, and a nose and white-lipped mouth appeared, distorted through the glass.

Death was looking in on him.

Felix shuddered and slipped his eyepatch back on, and the ghostly face disappeared. All that remained was an unaccountably odd pattern of rainwater against the windowpane.

Felix knew there were schemes hidden inside Death's dark stare. Schemes to entrap him, to keep him here forever, to lighten Death's load. He hid from that stare, for now at least, beneath his quilted bedcovers.

8
GRETCHEN

"GRETCHEN, FOR THE *last time*."

"Uhhh!" Gretchen groaned and threw down her soupspoon. It clanked against her bowl, then slipped into a watery grave of chicken broth.

"Heaven's sake," said Gram Whipple, "now look what you've done."

"It's not my fault," Gretchen protested. "This spoon is unmanageable."

"And are you also unmanageable?" said Gram. "No. You can manage your temper. You can manage your manners. Now take your soup to the kitchen and fetch a new bowl."

Gretchen grabbed her bowl from the table and trotted to the kitchen, where she fished out the sunken spoon and glared at the utensil—the source of all her woes.

She hadn't meant to slurp, hadn't realized she was being the least bit loud. But then her grandmother had made a big to-do about it three separate times, until the *last time*, when Gretchen had drowned the confounded spoon in a fit of rage. It wasn't fair to treat innocent cutlery like that, she knew. But it also wasn't fair that her grandmother picked and poked at Gretchen about every last thing she did.

Gretchen returned to the dining room, new bowl and spoon in hand. When she took her seat, something hard smacked into her shin, and Asa snickered at her from across the table.

"Stop kicking me," she hissed.

"Asa, stop kicking your sister," said Mayor Whipple distractedly, his voice a distant breeze.

Mayor Whipple was looking at a stack of papers propped to the side of his place setting. Important business. Occasionally, he would lift a sip of soup to his lips. Then he would blot his mouth and return to reading over his papers. It was infuriating. Gretchen wanted to stand up on her chair, storm across the table, and crash her foot into her father's food. She wanted to scream, "I'm here! *Your daughter.* Wake up, wake *up*!"

But Gretchen refrained from causing such a commotion, and Mayor Whipple didn't look up when she yelped at Asa kicking her other leg.

"Gretchen Marie!" cried Gram. "I'm not going to tell you again. You are thirteen. Act accordingly if you wish to attend the gala this year."

This wasn't a good threat on Gram's part. Gretchen had no desire to attend Boone Ridge's annual Christmas gala, an event that required her to wear itchy tights and a petticoat and shake the hands of all her father's boring friends.

Gretchen stared sullenly at her soup. A carrot floated by, then a chunk of celery. She spooned the carrot into her mouth and closed her lips in an awkward glom. She would not slurp, *she would not slurp*. Slowly, she squeaked the spoon from her mouth and set it back carefully in the bowl, slurp free. Gram Whipple did not notice this impressive feat. Her thoughts, it seemed, were wholly consumed by the Christmas gala; lately, it was all she talked about.

"I am not going to worry myself about you, Gretchen," she was saying. "I have a hundred and one other disasters to manage, from seating to flower arrangements."

"What's wrong with the flowers, Mom?" Mayor Whipple asked, still distracted by his papers. He reached over to pat her hand and, since he wasn't looking, patted the butter dish instead.

"Archie, really," said Gram, flicking his hand. "It's not that there is a problem at the florist but that there *will* be. It's the fate of any responsible soul who plans too well in advance. Misfortune always befalls the hard worker."

"Maybe you shouldn't plan so much then," suggested Gretchen.

She knew she was pressing her luck, but Gram was too distracted by future woes to notice her granddaughter's impertinence: "Poinsettias are a monstrously unpredictable flower. They possess an innate will to cause suffering in my life."

Gretchen was tempted to suggest that a simple solution would be to order flowers other than the accursed poinsettias. But that would be *too* impertinent, and Gretchen was not going to intentionally provoke her grandmother with the threat of North Carolina looming. She had to be on her best behavior, if not for her own sake, then for the case of Essie Hasting.

The questions writhed in Gretchen's mind, persistent little worms:

What did it mean, for Death to "kill" someone?

How was that any different from Death's usual job of taking people's lives?

Why would Death kill Essie Hasting?

And why—*why*—would Gretchen's father cover that up?

"Dad," Gretchen said.

It was the third time she'd said his name but the first time Mayor Whipple heard.

"Hm?" He looked up from his papers. "What is it?"

"Why do we hate the Hastings and the Vickeries?"

"Gretchen, really!" cried Gram. "Speaking those families' names in this house. Don't bother your father with such obscenities."

But it was too late. Gretchen had miraculously captured Mayor Whipple's attention.

"Curious question, Gretchen," he said. "What brings that on?"

Mayor Whipple was staring at her—not appalled like Gram, but staring all the same. Gretchen didn't blame either of them. The Whipples hated the Vickeries and the Hastings, and the Vickeries and the Hastings hated the Whipples. That's how it had been for time out of mind. No one spoke about that hate at the supper table; it simply *was*.

"I know why we hate them technically," said Gretchen. "Because they're apprentices, and they're no good. But no one ever talks about *why* they're no good."

"Don't answer her, Archie," Gram Whipple told her son. "It isn't appropriate."

Mayor Whipple was not listening to his mother. He was listening to Gretchen, for once. He leaned back, fingers interlocked. He seemed surprised, and more than a little amused.

"You know what apprentices do," he said.

"Sure. They live with Shades: Death, Memory, Passion. Help them out."

"Yes," said Mayor Whipple. "Like lackeys, groveling servants. They serve the Shades, and all for their own selfish reasons: the promise of a cure for some ailment, the erasure of memories too hard to bear, the hand of a love they cannot win on their own. They're too weak to seize such things for themselves, so they sign away their lives for a single favor. And so their loyalties lie with their Shades. But our loyalties lie—and always have—with the people first."

"Right. But the Vickeries help people, too. They're doctors."

"They are shams. They call themselves professionals, but they're as much doctors as Hemingway is a politician."

Hemingway was the family's cocker spaniel. He was fourteen years old, and his eyes perpetually leaked yellow goo.

"But then why do so many people in town go visit them?" Gretchen asked. "*They* seem to think the Vickeries are okay."

Mayor Whipple bristled, sitting up tall. "The Vickeries give them quick fixes, that's all. They *claim* they can save them from death, or take away all the bad memories in their heads. But death and memories, they catch up with you one way or another. All those towns-people will learn that lesson soon enough.

"*We* are really on the side of the people, Gretchen. Summoners—we maintain balance, you understand, among the three Shades, but also between them and humanity. In times of trouble, we intervene for our towns, using the Rites. We request miracles, memories, and love when our towns need them most. Ours is the noble task. A responsibility we have inherited for gener-ations."

Gretchen chose her next words carefully. She had her father's attention—a precious gift she did not mean to squander. "So, if Essie Hasting is dead, and Ms. Hasting is retired, who's going to be Passion's apprentice?"

Asa cussed, rubbing both hands over his cheeks and groaning low. "God, Gretch. Who dropped you on your head as an infant?"

"You, probably," she snapped at him.

"Passion will find another," Mayor Whipple said. "In this town of ours, there is no shortage of feeble characters to choose from. Three Shades to every town, one apprentice to each Shade, one summoner to balance and intercede using the Rites. That is the way of it. Always has been, and always will be."

The way Mayor Whipple spoke was not unkind, but it was worn, threadbare. Though Gretchen's father had never talked this much about the family business—not to Gretchen, a secondborn with no future in summoning—it sounded like a story he was exhausted of retelling. Gretchen could feel Gram firing an almighty glare in her direction, but she stayed the course.

"I go to school with a Vickery, you know. His name is Lee. Have you heard of him?"

"My dear, I barely have time to memorize the names of all my council members, let alone every member of your seventh-grade class."

"Eighth."

It wasn't Gretchen who'd corrected her father, but Asa. "She's in eighth grade, Dad."

Gretchen blinked, shocked first that *Asa* knew her grade, and second that he'd make any correction on her behalf.

"Very well, *eighth*. All the same, the Vickeries should be of no concern to you. Stay away from that boy."

"But *why*? I mean, how are they dangerous?"

"Their loyalties—"

"Yes, I know," Gretchen interrupted, earning a reproving look from Gram. "But what did they ever do to *us*?"

Mayor Whipple's brow creased, an expression Gretchen wasn't used to. Very rarely did her father look as though he were struggling for words. He always had a response on the tip of his tongue, ready for reporters and constituents and his family alike. But now, Mayor Whipple looked hesitant. Only after a long silence did he speak.

"We were born to be enemies. Apprentices might help the town in their way, but in the end they will always choose Shades first, and we will choose people. That is all there is to it. Some things in this life we simply must accept."

"But maybe," Gretchen said, "the apprentices know things we don't. Maybe we could learn from them."

She saw the precise moment she lost her father. His frank gaze closed, like double doors swinging shut. "Don't be absurd, Gretchen. Such thinking doesn't become a Whipple—even one like you, who will never practice." And like that, he was Mayor Whipple once more—the high summoner of Boone Ridge. "If you'll excuse me, I have five meetings tomorrow morning and a proposal I've only half read over."

He left the table without even touching dessert.

Asa was playing his music, volume cranked up high. The thumping bass made Gretchen's picture frames quiver on their nails, but she was used to it. After a while, she didn't even notice the wailing guitars.

Tonight, Gretchen sat on her window bench, looking out over Boone Ridge. Mayor Whipple had once told Gretchen that her room had the best view in the house. His window faced the industrial side of town, a place where down-and-out workers had swarmed during the Great Depression and that now looked like an even greater depression itself, all steel and sooty windows. Asa's window faced the back garden, and Gram's room had no windows at all.

But Gretchen's was the only bedroom that faced south, out toward the pretty end of Boone Ridge—a grid of quaint houses, fenced in and shaded by hickories. Gretchen could see Hickory Park, a black square tucked in amidst the houses. She couldn't see the police tape from so far away, but she knew it was still up, marking the place where Essie Hasting had died. And farther still in the distance rose a dark line of trees— Poplar Wood.

The wormy questions were back in Gretchen's mind, writhing and wriggling. They had grown in size and confidence, relentless. Together, they unearthed an idea inside her brain. It was an idea she could not shake, same as the poem she'd written on Mr. Edmonson's whiteboard.

She knew the Vickeries were her enemies. She knew they were bad. But just because you were an enemy did not mean you didn't *know things*. Things about Death. Things about Essie Hasting, another apprentice. Maybe, thought Gretchen, just maybe, if she was smart about it, her enemies would be willing to share those secrets, which was more than she could say of her own family.

A Whipple like you, who will never practice.

Her father's words stung inside Gretchen's ears, but she refused to accept them. With his help, or without it, she'd get to the bottom of this. She'd show her family just what a secondborn Whipple could do.

Gretchen needed her answers.

And so, she decided, she needed to speak to Lee Vickery.

9
LEE

"THE CHAMPION SITS with us!"

"Yeah, Lee, you hear that? Sit with us today."

Emma tugged Lee toward the only orange table in Boone Ridge Middle's cafeteria. It was a terrible table, rusty at the edges, riddled with chewing gum on its underside, and colored like a traffic cone. No one knew why this table wasn't green, like all the others in the cafeteria, but for that very reason it was where the popular kids had chosen to sit at the beginning of Lee's eighth-grade year, and it was, therefore, the coolest table in school.

This wasn't the first time Lee had been invited to the orange table. But unlike the other kids there, Lee never committed. Some days he chose to sit in the corner, with kids who wore all black. Other days he sat near the dessert cart, with the really smart kids. Some days he sat all alone, at the table next to the garbage cans. Lee didn't care where he sat, and for some reason that seemed to make him even cooler to the popular kids, which was why Emma and Dylan were so excitedly leading him along now.

"You guys," Dylan announced to the others seated at the orange table. "Lee here just set a new record. Forty-seven seconds around the entire field. He beat Chris Anding by a full *five*."

Lee reddened and took a seat next to Emma, who hadn't stopped smiling shyly at him since they'd left the recreational field.

"Dude," said one of the kids. "You're going to the Olympics for sure. Coach Rogers at the high school? He's going to put you on varsity track. My brother's on varsity too. He won the four-hundred-meter sprint at State."

"What're those, Lee?" asked Emma, pointing into his paper sack.

"Brownie bars. My mom made them yesterday. Want one?"

"You're so sweet!" Emma cried, grabbing the dessert from Lee's hand. "You should sit with us all the time."

Lee smiled and shrugged. If he were honest, he didn't like the kids at the orange table all that much.

They were loud and mean to each other, and the guys all wore a ton of gel in their hair. Lee worried that, if he were to sit with them every day, he'd have to start putting gel in his hair too. Also, he would much rather eat both his brownie bars than share.

"Hey, Lee," Dylan whispered across the table. "Don't look now, but Gretchen Whipple is totally staring at you."

Lee looked up from his pasta salad, half a noodle hanging out his mouth. Ashley Brown giggled at him. "Lee, you're *so adorable*."

Under the table, Emma clamped Lee's hand in a possessive grip. "Shut up, Ashley," she said.

Lee turned cautiously. Gretchen Whipple was sitting a few tables over with the girls' softball team, staring straight at him—until he stared straight back. Then her eyes widened, and she ducked her head.

"Man, she's got it bad," snickered Dylan. "Makes sense. Athletes go for each other."

"I'm not an athlete," said Lee at the same time Emma said, "Gretchen's not an athlete."

"She's. A. *Weirdo*," Emma went on, emphatically enunciating each word. "Sorry, but it's true. I heard Mayor Whipple had to bribe the principal not to expel her, just like he's had to for Asa. And did you hear what she did in Mr. Edmonson's class?"

"I was there," said Dylan. "The poem was stupid, but it was pretty great to see Mr. E flip out like that."

Lee was still looking at Gretchen. He knew that, unlike Dylan suggested, she most certainly did *not* have the hots for him—judging from the way she'd yelled at him Halloween night.

"Seriously, Lee, how do you run that fast? What's your secret?" asked Ashley.

"Uh," said Lee. "I just let my feet do all the work, you know? I've been running since I can remember. I time myself, and then I try to beat that time, then beat *that* time. So . . . that's how I do it."

Lee wasn't telling the whole truth. It was Felix who did the timing.

"Do you run a lot in the wood?" Emma asked. "I bet it's really peaceful out there."

Actually, Lee wanted to say, *it's more creepy than peaceful*. But he answered, "Sure, it's nice."

"Maybe we could hang out there sometime?" pressed Emma.

Lee pretended he had not heard the question. The Vickeries weren't encouraged to entertain guests who weren't patients. That wasn't part of the Agreement; it was simply understood that Death did not like visitors hanging about the place. Once, one of Lee's teachers had come for a house call and mistakenly knocked on the east end's door, then tripped and broken her wrist on the front porch—an "accident" Lee knew was Death's doing.

"I've heard your parents are pretty cool," said Dylan. "My mom saw your dad once about this sore throat that wouldn't go away, and she was better by the time she got home. But I bet your parents get in a lot of fights. Like, do they ever try to diagnose each other with diseases?"

"My mom's a psychiatrist," Lee said. "She listens to people more than anything else."

"Maybe Gretchen should make an appointment," Emma said, twirling her finger beside her head.

Lee just concentrated on eating his pasta salad.

When school was over, Lee left through the back exit. He didn't ride the bus or wait to be picked up—the Vickeries did not own a car. He walked home, cutting across the rec field toward Poplar Wood.

Today, Lee was halfway across the field when something hard whacked him on the back.

"Ow. What the—?"

Lee stumbled, nearly falling flat on his face. He turned to find that his attacker was none other than Gretchen Whipple.

"Hey," she said, far too casually.

"Uh, ow?" Lee rubbed at the space between his shoulder blades.

"Oh, stop. It was just a tap."

Lee backed away. "I shouldn't be talking to you."

Gretchen smiled. "And *I* shouldn't be talking to *you.*"

Lee backed farther away. Maybe the kids at the orange table were right about Gretchen. Staring at people and hitting them—maybe she really wasn't all there.

"What do you want?" he asked.

Gretchen was squinting at him as though trying to determine whether or not he was a spelling error. "What do you know about Essie Hasting?"

"What? Nothing."

"But you were at the burial."

"I told you, Felix and I always cut through the cemetery on our way to town."

"So that's his name! *Zeke* is really *Felix.* And where is he now?"

"He went back home." Lee turned red at his slip-up and redder still at his lie. "He's not in town anymore."

"Oh. Well, I do feel bad about what happened. I didn't know about his eye."

Lee was tense. Why was Gretchen Whipple speaking to him? Was she trying to trick him somehow? Judith had warned Lee that the Whipples were selfish and cunning.

"I can't talk to you," said Lee. "My mom wouldn't like it."

"Or is it because you have something to hide?" Gretchen took a step closer. "I think you know more about Essie Hasting than you're letting on. She was an apprentice, like you're going to be. You *have* to know more."

"I don't!" cried Lee. "You think just because I was around her funeral means I know something? It doesn't work that way. I didn't hang out with the Hastings. I didn't know them at all."

"I need your help," said Gretchen.

"What?" Lee was positive he hadn't heard her right.

"I'm investigating something," she said, matter-of-factly. "It might get me into trouble, so I've got to have help."

"But why are you asking *me*? I'm an apprentice."

"Not technically," said Gretchen. "You're not a true apprentice until you sign your contract. That is, if you decide to sign at all." She smirked at Lee's startled expression. "Yeah. I've done my research."

"Well that . . . doesn't change anything! You're still a summoner."

"Ugh," said Gretchen. "Get *over* it, would you? I'm being very open-minded, Vickery. Why not show me the same courtesy?"

"Because your family is rotten. All you want is money and power, and you don't care who you hurt to get it." Lee was surprised by the words coming from his mouth—accusations rolling out like clunking marbles. They were all *true* words, of course. Judith had told him those things, and she was not a liar.

Gretchen gripped her arms more tightly against her chest. "Fine. You wanna think that about me? Go right ahead. I won't say all the horrible things I know about *your* family."

"Like what?"

"For one thing, you're sellouts. You do whatever the Shades ask, no matter how bad. *Lackeys.* That's what my dad calls you."

Lee's heart began to pound.

"*But,*" said Gretchen, "I'm willing to overlook that, because this is bigger than Vickeries or Whipples."

"What is?"

Gretchen heaved in a big breath and said, "Death killed Essie Hasting."

Lee stared. "What do you mean? Death kills everyone."

"No," said Gretchen. "Not *took her life.* Death *killed* Essie. Before her appointed time. And I'm trying to figure out why."

Lee didn't know what to think. Only Felix and his mother spoke about Shades. To hear Gretchen say Death's name, as though Death were a real person, was strange enough. But what Gretchen's words meant— that was even stranger.

"If Death did anything," Lee said slowly, "I wouldn't know. I live with Memory, not him."

Gretchen's eyes flashed with doubt. "I thought you lived with both of them?"

"Well." Lee's ears were hot. "I do, I guess. Technically. But it's . . ."

"It's what?"

He felt sure his eardrums were now on fire and would soon catch his whole body alight. He wasn't supposed to talk to Whipples, and he definitely wasn't supposed to talk to them about the Agreement, or Felix, or *any* of this. If Gretchen Whipple was attempting to trick him into revealing secrets, she was doing a very good job.

Lee was beginning to feel guilty, even though he was certain he had nothing to be guilty about. He couldn't stick around longer, for fear of what else Gretchen Whipple might do. So he ran. He set off at full speed for Poplar Wood and looked back just once to see if Gretchen was following.

She hadn't moved an inch. She stood in the middle of the rec field, shoulders drooped, as though she had lost a fight.

Death had killed Essie Hasting?

Death had *killed* Essie Hasting?

If that was true, then what did Felix know?

Forty-seven seconds. Lee was sure he could beat that record now.

10
FELIX

Just as Felix had predicted, true November finally arrived. Warmth was gone for good. Bitter cold stiffened the air, and the Vickery twins could no longer meet comfortably on the front porch. Instead, they moved to the back of the house—a narrow porch, fully enclosed in glass and furnished with a cast-iron stove.

Their mother called this place the conservatory. The west end of the porch was filled with crawling vines, orchids, and a wild breed of flower that came from the Amazon. The east end was filled with nothing but dust and dirt.

Today, Lee sat in a wicker chair, studying for a history exam. Felix lay on his back, studying the stem of a white orchid. They had passed half an hour like this, in calm quiet. Some days the brothers did not talk, merely kept each other company.

Felix had just stretched his legs and was readying to return to work, when there was a terrible *crash!* He ducked, and something smashed into the potted orchid behind him.

"We're under attack!" shouted Lee, shielding his face with A *Survey of World History.*

When Felix righted himself, he was staring straight through broken glass at a girl. Her hair was black as soot, and her lips were a startling shade of red. She was clearly the source of the flying ball, and she was *smiling.* It was the same girl who had yelled at him on Halloween. Gretchen Whipple.

"Oops," she said, smiling big. "It looks like I've damaged your property with my softball. Aren't you going to invite me in so I can make amends?"

Felix removed the book draped over Lee's face.

"What's she doing here?" he whispered.

But Lee looked as startled as Felix felt.

"I'm coming in!" said Gretchen.

She sprinted up the conservatory steps and burst in. Shards of glass crunched beneath her sneakers, and the closer she drew to Felix, the farther he drew away.

"You again!" she said. "You remember me, don't you?"

Felix remembered. He remembered Gretchen's shout of disgust when she'd ripped back his eyepatch. He remembered very well.

"Why don't you run away?" Felix said, his heel backing into the wall. "Isn't that what you're supposed to do when you break a window?"

"I'm the mayor's daughter, Zeke. I've got honor." She stepped nearer, closing the distance. "But I know your name isn't really Zeke. It's Felix. Your friend Lee here told me, didn't you, Lee?"

Lee sputtered. His eyes were wide with horror.

"Actually," said Gretchen, reflecting, "you told me he'd gone back home. And now he's here, at your house. So either he's back *again,* or you lied. Who are you really, Felix? Some kind of relative?"

Gretchen looked him over, then looked over Lee. "You don't look a thing alike," she decided aloud. "By the way, Lee, why do you Vickeries even live out here? Aren't you afraid of getting poison ivy, like, all the time? Or getting attacked by bears? I hear bears live out here."

"There aren't any bears," said Felix. "And you don't have to worry about poison ivy unless you're a complete idiot and don't know how to spot it."

"I guess that's something you'll have to teach me, Felix. I'm sure we'll be spending a lot of time together from now on."

"What's she talking about?" Felix asked Lee.

"How should I know!" cried Lee, again covering his face with the book.

"Felix," said a booming voice. "What's going on out here?"

Felix turned around. His father was in the doorway.

"This girl broke the window!" he said. "And now she won't leave."

"Ha!" Gretchen shoved past Felix. "Finally, an adult. You're Vince Vickery, right?"

She thrust her hand out. Vince shook it quite calmly, given the circumstances, and said, "Correct."

"Well 'this girl' happens to be Gretchen Whipple. I'm Mayor Whipple's daughter."

Vince's expression remained unchanged. "I see."

"I came in to make amends for my destructive behavior," Gretchen said.

"Very well. I'd estimate that a new pane would cost about—"

"Oh, no! No, I can't *pay* you for it. I don't have that kind of money, and I can't tell my father or Gram. I'd rather die. You know, seeing how you all are *Vickeries*."

"Well," said Vince. "That puts us in something of a pickle, doesn't it?" To Felix's annoyance, his father looked rather amused by Gretchen. Hadn't he heard her? She was a *Whipple*. Whipples were the *enemy*. Vince had told Felix so himself.

"Oh no, it doesn't," said Gretchen. "See, I might not have the money, but I've got plenty of free time. I'm the smartest kid in my class, so I finish all my homework at lightning speed. That means I could make up the cost of repairs in manual labor. You all would like that, right? A Whipple doing chores for you? I'm sure I could be a big help to Lee and his friend here."

Vince stiffened. "Lee?" he said quietly.

"Well, *yeah.*" Gretchen flapped her arm in Lee's general direction.

A cold sadness crept over Felix. Lee had lowered his history book and was staring hard at the place where Vince stood. Lee and his father couldn't see each other, of course; that was part of the Agreement. But somehow, *somehow,* Lee always seemed to sense when his father was near. He now stood still as a wax figurine. Vince stood motionless, too.

"Uh," said Gretchen. "Everything okay?"

Vince shook his head. "Yes, excuse me. Everything is fine."

"Uh-huh. So, what'll it be? Hard labor in the attic? Yard work? Window washing? I'll make it up however you see fit. I'd just prefer you didn't tell my father about this little incident. I would be grounded for*ever* if he found out I'd been hanging around here."

Vince narrowed his eyes at Gretchen. "And would you care to explain *why* you've been hanging around here?"

89

Finally, thought Felix. *He's taking this seriously.*

"Oh." Gretchen's fingers fidgeted. "I'm not a spy or anything, if that's what you think! I won't report all your secrets back home, promise."

Vince knelt so he was on her level. "I'm not sure what you're up to, Miss Whipple, but trust me, whatever it is, it's unwise. You may be rebelling against your father—that's to be expected at your age—but you should not do so here. It's dangerous."

The way Gretchen's face lit up, Felix suspected his father had said the exact wrong thing. But quickly, she shifted her features into something like outrage. "What?! I've got to make up for the damage somehow!"

Vince rose to his feet. "There's nothing for you to do. Now be off to town, Miss Whipple, before the wood grows dark."

"This . . . floor! It's filthy! I could clean that for you!"

Vince's face tightened around the lips. It was an expression that Felix only ever saw him wear in one other situation, whenever Death stood at the foot of a patient's bed—a sign that the patient was fated to die.

"Leave this property, Miss Whipple," he said, firm. "I will cover the cost of the glass, and I don't want to hear from you again. You or any of your family."

"I *am* sorry about the window. The plants aren't going to die, are they?" Gretchen pointed to the orchids, and to the Amazonian flower.

"I'm sure my wife will see that they don't."

In that moment, Vince looked so infinitely sad that Felix had to look away. When he looked back, his father was gone, the screen door latched behind him. He turned on Gretchen. "You planned this, didn't you? You threw that ball *on purpose.*"

Gretchen sniffed, staring at the closed door. "I wanted to practice my pitching."

Felix's father had warned him that the Whipples were not to be trusted. They did anything, fooled anyone, to get what they wanted.

Lee had shaken from his frozen state and was now glaring hard at Gretchen. "Is this about Essie Hasting?" he asked. "I told you I don't know anything."

"YOU DO," cried Gretchen, pointing at both of them. "And I'm going to get the truth out of you Vickeries, whether you like it or not!"

With that, Gretchen Whipple flung open the conservatory door and stomped away.

"What . . . just happened?" whispered Lee.

"Not a clue." Felix turned to his brother. "Why didn't you tell me she'd talked to you?"

"I . . . hadn't gotten the chance."

"She's a *Whipple*."

"Yeah, well, I didn't think she'd come out here and throw stuff at us. I don't even know what she wants."

Felix peered through the frame of broken glass, watching Gretchen disappear into the wood. "Me neither. But I'm pretty sure she means business."

11

GRETCHEN

GRETCHEN'S PLAN WAS working, though maybe not *exactly* as she'd intended. For one thing, she hadn't expected that Felix boy to be at the house. For another, she'd thought the Vickeries would be much angrier about the broken window and insist on at least a week's worth of hard labor to make up for the damage. And she certainly hadn't expected that meeting Vince Vickery— an *actual apprentice*—would be so scary. She wondered if any of them had seen her hands shaking.

The last thing Gretchen had not counted on was getting lost in Poplar Wood. It had taken her a full hour to find Poplar House, and she'd wondered the whole way why, what with so many patients who visited the

Vickeries, there wasn't a path that led to the front door. Did every patient have to forge their way through this wood? Was it a test of fortitude they had to pass in order to receive treatment?

Of course, Gretchen had been very careful about it and tied strips of Gram's knitting yarn around the trees as she went so she could trace her steps back. The trouble was, Gretchen hadn't seen a single one of her yarn-marked trees in the last ten minutes, and now dusk was coming on. If she wasn't home for dinner, Gram would throw a fit.

"See?" she said out loud to the listening wood. "This is why Gram should let me get a cell phone. I might die in this wood, and all because I couldn't call for help."

It was a poor argument, and Gretchen knew it. Gram had told Gretchen that she couldn't have a phone until her fifteenth birthday, but she had also strictly forbidden Gretchen from ever going into Poplar Wood. Gram wouldn't be convinced to give Gretchen a phone just so that Gretchen could more conveniently disobey her rules.

But Gram wasn't here, and the trees were not arguing with Gretchen's logic, so she kept on talking: "Half of eighth grade already has one! Maybe if Gram weren't from, like, the sixteenth century, she wouldn't—"

"Who are you talking to, crazy?"

Gretchen shrieked. A tall, snickering boy emerged from behind an oak.

"Asa," Gretchen gasped. Asa just snickered some more, but Gretchen was a little glad he'd appeared. "What are you doing out here?"

"Could ask you the same question. Gram is going to be so pissed at you."

"You can't say anything to her. *Please*. She'll ground me for weeks."

Asa just hocked up a wad of spit and aimed it into the underbrush. "Should've thought of that before you came in here. Just what were you doing, Gretch?"

"None of your business. And I didn't mean to get lost. I left a trail, I just couldn't find it again."

"What, you mean this?" Asa unzipped one of his leather jacket's many pockets and pulled out a handful of yarn pieces.

Gretchen gaped. "You *followed* me?"

"My little sister was sneaking out her bedroom window without telling Gram where she was going." Asa smiled, all wrong. "I was worried about her."

"You were not! Why would you do that to me?"

"You weren't really lost. I just thought it'd be funny to see how bad your sense of direction is, and let me tell you, it's *bad*. You don't hold up well under pressure."

Gretchen shoved at Asa's gut. Asa didn't budge.

"You weren't even in trouble," he said. "Come on, I'll drive you back home."

Gretchen folded her arms and stayed where she was. "I'll walk."

"But you'll be late for dinner."

"You're such a jerk, Asa. I'm going to tell—"

"Who?" Asa smiled an even worse smile than before. "Gram? You going to tell her you were hanging around *Poplar House*?"

"I hate you," Gretchen said.

"Whatever." Asa pointed through the trees. "We're only a minute from the main road. You were fine all along."

Just as Asa said, the main road was less than a minute's walk away, and so was his motorbike. When they reached it, he mounted and nodded at Gretchen to do the same.

"I'm not riding without a helmet," she said. "And you shouldn't, either."

Asa gave Gretchen a look that made her feel like a stick-in-the-mud. But he dismounted, threw open the bike seat, and tossed a helmet right at Gretchen's face. Luckily, softball had made her a good catch.

They didn't speak to each other on the ride home. Even if Gretchen had wanted to talk to her brother, she wouldn't have been heard over the roar of the engine as Asa drove straight through four-way stops, weaving from lane to lane.

When they reached Carver Street, Asa kept driving straight, passing it by. What was he thinking? Carver Street was by far the fastest route home. It was a quick flash by Hickory Park, a turn onto Main Street, and another turn onto Avenue B that led straight up to their doorstep—a five-minute ride at most. It was strange that Asa had missed the turn, but stranger still that he missed Clay Street, and Calhoun after it.

"What are you doing?!" Gretchen shouted, but Asa did not answer.

At this rate, thought Gretchen, they would miss Hickory Park altogether. And that, in fact, was precisely what they did. Asa turned up Gregory Street, a stretch of brick apartments that was a full block past the park. Gretchen didn't try to speak again until they arrived at the gated driveway of the mayor's house.

"Why'd you take such a long way home?"

"What're you talking about?" said Asa, wheeling his bike to the garage.

"You went all the way around Hickory Park."

"So what? The park's an eyesore. All that yellow tape."

Gretchen frowned at her brother. He smiled an ugly smile.

Dinner passed in silence, punctuated only by the clink of silverware and the occasional request for a dish. Asa said nothing, as usual. Mayor Whipple, too busy with a stack of business-related documents, said nothing, as usual. Gram said nothing, aside from the occasional reprimand that Gretchen remove her elbows from the table, Gretchen not slurp so loud, Gretchen take smaller bites—as usual.

Everything was as it always was, but Gretchen felt different. She had visited the house in Poplar Wood. She'd asked the *Vickeries* for help. She wondered if anyone could see that on her face, see a change in the way she ate—poking at her food but putting little in her mouth.

Mayor Whipple stood abruptly, gathering his stack of papers.

"Archie, *really*," said Gram. "You can't wait for dessert? Cobbler tonight."

"Sorry, Mom. Business."

Business.

That was the excuse Mayor Whipple used, whether he was leaving the supper table or missing one of Gretchen's softball games. In front of the family, business was papers and phone calls and finely dressed houseguests. But Gretchen knew there was more to it than that. There was plenty of business her father did in his home office, with the doors shut and locked. Business, she assumed, that had to do with the Shades.

Most nights after dinner, Gretchen would lock herself in her bedroom, where she'd do her homework or read a book. Tonight, she had other plans. She walked down the long, wood-paneled hallway, toward her father's office. The double doors were shut tight, as Gretchen expected. That meant her father was not to be disturbed, and Gretchen did not mean to disturb him. She only meant to eavesdrop.

When it came to eavesdropping, Gretchen considered herself an expert. She'd listened in on her father's meetings since she was a little girl. There was a perfect spot for it—in the family library, the room adjacent to Mayor Whipple's office, in the narrow slip of wall between two mahogany bookshelves. There, Gretchen pressed the drinking glass to the wall and her ear to the glass, and listened.

When she'd been much smaller—seven or eight— Gretchen had eavesdropped for the fun of it. Back then, the secrets themselves did not interest her. They were usually about council reports and campaigns and other political matters, conversations between her father and old, boring men—members of the city council and occasionally a lawyer or a judge, who spoke in jabbering legalese Gretchen could not understand.

But the older Gretchen got, the more she understood. Sometimes, even now, she found the secrets boring—talk of new traffic lights and building codes. But there were interesting topics, too—talk of allowing certain people out of jail on good behavior, or of paying the editor of the *Boone Herald* to print a particular headline.

Gretchen had always liked the thrill, the intrigue. But—thrilling as it was—she hadn't liked what she'd heard the Tuesday before, about Essie Hasting. Since then, she'd listened at this wall every night, hoping her father might talk of it more, and leave some hint as to what he'd meant when he'd told the sheriff and coroner that Death killed Essie *for reasons of his own.* So far, she'd been out of luck. It was back to tax cuts and demolition permits and the regular rigmarole of town affairs.

But, Gretchen reminded herself, real-life mysteries weren't always glamorous. She was sure Sherlock Holmes had lots of boring days. And it would take more than a week of building code discussions to deter Gretchen Whipple.

Tonight, her father's office was quiet. Gretchen listened for a minute, and another. There was rustling—the clank of metal and the thud of something heavy. Then, more silence. Gretchen sighed, impatient. She could endure the mundane, yes, but that didn't mean she had to be happy about it.

Another minute passed, and then her father spoke. His words came out in an even patter, as though Mayor Whipple was quoting a poem. He was murmuring too low for Gretchen to make out the words themselves. Still, she waited, and at last she heard words she could understand.

"What do you want from me?"

Her father was speaking at a normal volume now, *louder* than a normal volume. It sounded like he was talking to someone on the phone.

"I know the terms," Mayor Whipple went on. "I'm not interfering. I've done nothing. *Less* than nothing. I called everyone off your scent, what more do you want?"

Questions and possibilities sparked in Gretchen's head. Was someone blackmailing her father? Was—

"What do you think you're doing, you little snoop?"

"AAAH!"

Gretchen lost hold of the glass, and it landed on the carpet with a soft *thump*. She turned and looked up at Asa and tried to spit out an excuse.

"I'm not—that's not—I don't really—"

An excuse was not coming. It didn't matter, really.

"Listening in on Dad?" Asa asked, grinning that awful grin.

It would be very silly to insist that she wasn't.

"I *wasn't*." Gretchen immediately felt very silly.

Asa picked up the fallen glass. "Private business is *private*."

"Easy for you to say. You get to know everything, *do* everything. Dad's told you all the family secrets."

"You seem to think that's a good thing."

"It *is*! And you all don't tell me anything, so I have to figure it out for myself. Just because I'm the secondborn doesn't mean I'm not smart. I could do the same things as you; I know it. I could summon, too!"

Asa gripped the glass, the veins of his hand bulging. "You don't know what you're after. Summoning, Rites—they aren't what you think."

"How do you know what I think?"

"'*Dad*,'" said Asa, in a high-pitched imitation of Gretchen's voice. "'What if we can *learn* from the Vickeries? Why can't we all get along?'"

"That's not how I sound."

"But it's what you asked. You believe all that crap about us using the Rites for the good of Boone Ridge. But that's not what they're for. That's not what *Dad* uses them for. Believe me, you don't want to know the real family business."

"I *do*, though."

"Well, I'm not talking about it."

"You're the one who brought it up!"

Asa said nothing, only tapped the base of the drinking glass. Gretchen decided on another approach.

"Asa?" she said, very soft. "Have you ever done it? Summoned with a Rite?"

Asa did not look surprised by the question. He didn't look angry, or particularly anything. "Why do you care?"

"I just want answers, that's all. I've got to get them someplace. And it's not like I can touch the Book of Rites."

She'd done it now. She'd said the words: Book of Rites.

They were a matter of feet from it as they spoke. On a bronze pedestal, beneath one of the library's tall, stained-glass windows, there rested a locked glass case, and within that case sat an open book. Its title was gold leaf, its pages brittle, its illustrations sepia. It was the Book of Rites, the oldest book the Whipple family owned. The book with which they summoned. The book that, according to their father, had made the Whipple family what it was today.

Asa looked Gretchen straight in the eye. "Maybe you don't think so now but you're lucky you're secondborn. Stay away from that book, if you know what's good for you. Stay away from all of it."

Gretchen opened her mouth, but Asa was gone, having taken with him her tried-and-true eavesdropping glass. Still, Gretchen returned to the wall and pressed her ear close, trying to hear. She listened, waited, for minutes. There was not even a hint of sound. Whatever conversation her father had been having was over now, and Gretchen was left alone, with no secrets gained and a dozen new suspicions.

12
LEE

"How long has she been out there?"

"An hour, maybe? I don't know."

"Why is she sweeping?"

Lee looked at his mother and made a queasy face. "She may have mentioned manual labor?"

It was Saturday, the morning after Gretchen Whipple's surprise appearance at Poplar House, and she was back. She was in the conservatory and, of all things, she was *sweeping the floor*. Every so often, she would duck her mouth into the crook of her arm and cough, then look around as though expecting someone to show up. In fact, Lee had accidentally discovered Gretchen's presence, when he'd headed to the conservatory to do some reading for school. He'd frozen in place at the sight of her, then run into the parlor to alert Judith. Now they stood watching her through the back door.

Judith had been angry enough the day before, when she'd learned about the conservatory window. She'd been angrier still to learn that a *Whipple* had done it.

"I don't know what Archibald is about, sending his youngest child to vandalize our property," she'd said. "We've kept ourselves at a mutually agreeable distance all this time. There's no need for him to be such a malicious coward, as though he wanted to *start* something. As though we'd stoop to the level of Hatfields and McCoys!"

Lee winced. Of course he knew about the Hatfields and McCoys—two feuding families of old who lived farther east. Most ordinary people knew about that feud, but very few knew the real reason for it—that the Hatfields were summoners and the McCoys apprentices. The way Judith told the story, the McCoys had of course been in the right.

Lee didn't have the heart to tell his mother that Gretchen's vandalism wasn't Mayor Whipple's fault but Lee's own. Gretchen was after *him*, and he was starting to suspect she wasn't going to give up until he agreed to help her with her ridiculous mystery—which, he had a feeling, would only entangle their families all the more.

"I've no idea what that child is up to," Judith said now, "but she must leave immediately. Go and tell her."

"But she won't! You don't know how stubborn she is."

"And how do *you* know that?" His mother fixed him with narrowed, probing eyes.

Lee swallowed and shrugged. "She goes to my school is all. I see her around."

"If this continues, I'll have no choice but to go into town and speak to Mayor Whipple in person. It's simply—"

"No!" Lee blurted, turning very red. "Don't talk to Mayor Whipple. Don't . . . start a fight or anything. I'll—I'll take care of it."

And with that, determined not to become yet another McCoy, Lee headed out to the porch. The door clattered behind him, and Gretchen whirled around, brandishing her plastic broom like a softball bat. Lee shielded his face.

"Whoa, *whoa!* It's just me!"

"Sheesh!" said Gretchen. "I'm not going to hit you."

"You sure look like it!"

Gretchen seemed to notice the aggressive position of her broom then, and lowered it. "Sorry. I was starting to think no one was home."

"We're almost always home."

"Oh, so you guys saw me out here, *toiling away* for my misdeed, and just decided to be rude."

"If anyone's being rude," said Lee, "it's you. You weren't supposed to come back here."

"I see the window's patched up." Gretchen motioned with her broom to the plywood-covered hole. It hadn't taken Judith too long to devise a temporary repair, and the glassworker was supposed to come on Monday. "Still think I broke it on purpose?" she asked, looking strangely pleased.

"Who knows." Lee shrugged. "Felix definitely thinks so."

"Well, he's smart. I did." She swept a little more, then stopped to give Lee a hard stare. "Does Felix live here?"

"Uh. Well." Lee tried to conjure a plausible lie, but all that came out was "I guess so."

"What do you mean, you 'guess so'? Either he does or he doesn't. Is he visiting from out of town, or what?"

"None of your business." Lee didn't like how he sounded. He wasn't normally mean. Was it just Gretchen who brought the mean out? Because she was a Whipple?

"Gosh, you're snippy," she said. "And to think, I'm cleaning your dirty floor."

"No one asked you to clean it. You were told to *stay away.*"

"I'm not very good with rules. Anyway, I wouldn't have had to come back if you'd given me the right answer the first time."

"I did give you an answer," Lee said.

"Not the *right* one. And then you ran away. Really fast, I might add. You're, like, abnormally fast. Has anyone told you that?"

"Yeah," Lee muttered.

"Well, aren't we proud! Just because you've sat at the orange table a few times doesn't mean you've got the right to be all high and mighty."

"Just leave, would you?" Lee cried, exasperated. "My brother and I don't want anything to do with your stupid murder mystery!"

Gretchen's eyes got big, and she shrieked, "HA!"

"W-what?"

"Your brother?" she said. "Your *brother*?!"

Lee felt his face go hot.

"What?" he said. "I meant—"

"So he *is* your brother! You really don't look a thing alike, though. And how come he doesn't come to school? How come I never see him around? Are your parents trying to hide him away? Is it because of—" Gretchen grew solemn and whispered, "Is it because of his eye?"

"What about my eye?"

Lee had been so panicked about slipping up he hadn't noticed Felix standing at the east-end door.

Gretchen, too, was so startled that she dropped her broom. "Oh," she said. "Sorry. Hello."

Felix remained behind the screen.

"I was born half blind," he said. "There's nothing wrong with that."

"No, no! Of course not." Gretchen suddenly looked out of sorts. "I didn't say there was anything wrong. I didn't even know before, at the bonfire, I swear I didn't, or I wouldn't have—"

"Looked ready to puke at the sight of me? Sure. I get it."

"I'm half deaf!" Lee blurted. He didn't know how else to make up for the mess he'd created.

Gretchen turned on him with a curious expression. "Really?"

"Yeah, really." He tapped his left ear. "Since birth. It's part of the Agreement."

"What Agreement?"

"Lee," said Felix, warningly. "Shut up."

Lee wondered if he should just go out into the wood, dig a hole, and hide there until Gretchen left. She had an awful way of making him say things he shouldn't.

"What Agreement?" Gretchen pressed excitedly. "Agreement with whom? About what?"

"That's none of your business," said Felix, pushing into the conservatory, arms crossed.

"I can keep a secret!" Gretchen pleaded. "I swear, I wouldn't tell anyone. I don't have any friends to tell secrets *to*!"

"It's not—"

But here, Lee stopped short. There was a cold breeze blowing against his unhearing ear—a breath, and words slipped out upon it.

"She is not wanted here."

Felix had raised his eyepatch and was staring behind Lee, at something Lee could not see but Felix could, and something that Felix could not hear but Lee could.

Death was standing in the conservatory.

"What Agreement?" Gretchen asked again. "Did your parents make a deal with the devil, or what?"

"Gretchen," said Felix, "you need to go."

"She could disappear so easily," whispered lips at Lee's ear. *"A mere snuff or a snip, a wrong gust of the wind, and her wick would be out. If she snoops around places she should not go, such a premature end might be her fate."*

Felix looked at Lee. "What is he saying?"

"What's *who* saying?" Gretchen looked between the brothers. "You two are starting to creep me out."

"Little girls should not be investigating deaths. What happened in Hickory Park is my business. Mine alone."

"Felix is right," said Lee, trying to keep his voice from shaking. "You need to go. Now."

"Come on, just say you'll help me! Then I'll go."

Lee could hear Death moving away from him and closer to Gretchen. Felix had gone white in the face.

"Such a shame to do away with a candle that tall and bright. And a summoner, too. What a pity."

"Please, Gretchen, *leave*," Lee pleaded.

Suddenly, Gretchen cried out and fell backward against the conservatory door. Its latch gave way, and she tumbled down the steps.

Felix shouted, and Lee followed after him down to where Gretchen lay, still and silent on the frosted ground. She did not stir. She did not speak. Her eyes were closed.

"What did you do?" Felix shouted at the air.

But a low voice on the porch steps said, "*Consider that a warning*," and Lee felt cold air move across the back of his neck. Death was gone.

Gretchen's eyes fluttered open. "Ow." Slowly, she sat up, rubbing her right elbow. "*Owww*. I think I broke something."

The brothers sighed, relieved.

Then Felix said, "It's your own fault for coming here."

Lee nudged him. "She's actually *hurt*." He turned to Gretchen. "If you've broken something, our dad should look at you. Do you, uh, think you can walk?"

Gretchen made a face, but she nodded, and with Lee's help she got to her feet, leaning against him as he helped her up the conservatory steps.

Felix followed, wary. "This . . . this isn't a good idea. Death doesn't want her here. He said he wants her to leave."

"But she's not a trespasser anymore," said Lee. "She's a patient. Death can't harm her for that. Now come on."

As he helped Gretchen, step by step, to the east-end door, Lee began to laugh.

"What's so funny?" Felix asked.

"I don't know."

None of this was funny at all, really. It was just that Lee couldn't help but think this was exactly the sort of thing Gretchen had wanted to happen.

13
FELIX

"A SPRAINED ELBOW."

That was Vince Vickery's professional medical conclusion, but from the way Gretchen moaned and groaned, Felix would have guessed she'd been torn into a hundred thousand pieces.

"Shouldn't there be a preacher present?" she whimpered from the examination table. "Aren't I supposed to get my last rites?"

"You're not going to die," said Felix. "Stop being dramatic."

"Well don't you have a fine bedside manner?" Gretchen whined. "Why can't Lee be in here? He'd be nicer at least."

"Dad . . . banned him from the examination room. He got into the herbs one time and mixed them all up, trying to make his own medicine. It took Dad forever to sort them back out."

Felix was rather impressed with his lie under pressure.

Gretchen, however, was not. "What if your dad's wrong and I've been torn up inside? What if my spleen has, like, exploded? What if I hit my head so hard that something is loose up there?"

"It didn't, and it isn't. My dad is never wrong."

That was true enough. Vince was never wrong, because *Death* was never wrong. He had followed them into the examination room and, while Vince checked Gretchen over for injuries, had stood behind her head. When Death stood at the head of the table, there was nothing to worry about. It was when he stood at the foot that the outcome was unalterable: the patient would die.

And even though it was only a sprain, and even though Death was on the good end of the table *today*, Felix felt a prickling all along his arms. Death had made it clear he did not want Gretchen to visit again. Even now, his ice-blue eyes were glazed with malice. He looked contemptuously at Gretchen, smoothing the lapels of his black jacket, even though his three-piece suit was never the least bit disheveled.

Felix placed the eyepatch back on his right eye. He had seen enough.

Minutes earlier, Vince had left the room with a handful of canisters, all filled with herbs. It was not difficult to boil a broth that soothed sprains—Felix knew the recipe by heart. But Vince had ordered him to remain in the examination room to keep Gretchen company.

Maybe it was punishment, Felix reflected, for letting Gretchen back on their property. But, he thought bitterly, it wasn't *his* fault. Gretchen had a will so strong that Death himself had had to intervene.

"I hope you've learned your lesson," Felix told Gretchen. "Now you know not to come poking around the house anymore. It isn't safe."

"Isn't safe?" Gretchen snorted. "You bet it isn't, with rickety stairs like that. Come to think of it, I could sue."

"Only you won't," Felix said, "because you don't want your dad finding out about any of this."

There. He had won this argument for sure.

"Fine," said Gretchen. "Maybe I won't sue. But that doesn't mean I won't keep bothering you. I'll come back to this house every day until the last Saturday of all eternity, until Lee agrees to help me. You're going to have to do more than sprain my elbow to keep me away."

"*I* didn't sprain your elbow. And it's against the law to bother people like that. There's such a thing as private property."

"So! I won't trespass. I'll just hide out in the wood and sing 'Rocky Top' at the top of my lungs, for hours straight."

Felix did not doubt that Gretchen would do just that. He wondered if maybe she wasn't winning the argument after all. He flipped up his eyepatch again to find that Death was no longer in the room. Most likely he was attending one of his many out-of-house appointments. Appointments that did not require a doctor's medicine or care. Appointments that only ever meant death.

Felix slid the eyepatch back in place and then, before Gretchen could make another threat, he ran to the kitchen, where his father was stooped over a boiling pot on the stovetop.

"Can't you finish any sooner?" Felix begged. "She's driving me crazy."

"Then you shouldn't have let her back here."

Now that Vince was out of Gretchen's presence—he was always calm and collected with his patients—he sounded severe.

"I didn't *let* her anywhere! She came back all on her own."

"She's upset Death."

"I know," Felix said miserably. "Lee said Death called it a 'warning.'"

"Then you'd better see to it that she stays away. Even if her motives are innocent—which I seriously doubt, given her parentage—she can't be hanging around."

Felix ignored the uneasy feeling in his gut. "Don't Whipples make their own deals with Death, though?" he asked. "Rites?"

The word tasted sour on his tongue. His father had taught him many years ago about Rites—the spells summoners performed to communicate with the Shades.

"It's clear Gretchen's father has made deals with him over the years," said Vince. "Perhaps even his son has, by now. But Gretchen's too young for that yet."

"But Death wouldn't . . . you know, *kill* her?"

Vince looked up sharply. "You know as well as I: Death can only take lives at their appointed time."

"I know, I know," Felix mumbled.

He really did know. He'd witnessed enough deaths in his thirteen years. And the truth was, not all of those deaths had been bad. Some were even peaceful. Some patients, old and worn by decades, passed on with accepting smiles, loved ones holding their hands.

Felix knew this was how Death worked—taking lives only when their time had come.

Still, he could not shake the image of Death's angered eyes, just before he pushed Gretchen down the conservatory stairs. He'd looked . . . *murderous*. As though this were not a matter of appointed times, but of something far more personal.

"Here." Vince handed Felix a clay bowl, hot with freshly boiled broth, and then placed a hand on his shoulder.

"She can't return to this house," he said. "You must make sure of that."

Felix nodded. He cupped the bowl in his gloved hands and carried it back to the examination room, prepared to face Gretchen once more.

"Okay," he said, walking in. "You've got to drink it all down, or—"

Felix stopped short. He looked around.

Gretchen was gone.

14
GRETCHEN

SHE HAD ESCAPED through the window.

Gretchen had had her fill of sitting in that cold room, arguing with an impossible boy named Felix when she'd really only come there for an impossible boy named Lee. So she'd seized her chance and left.

Her right arm was throbbing like the bass in one of Asa's heavy metal songs, but that was nothing Gretchen couldn't endure with a little teeth-gritting. So she gritted her teeth especially hard and tumbled out the window and into the conservatory, bonking her injured elbow into an unexpected object.

"Ow," said the object, which turned out to be Lee.

"What're you standing outside the window for?" Gretchen asked him. "That's super creeperly of you."

"Ow," Lee said again, rubbing at his jaw.

"Felix says you're not allowed in there. That true?"

Lee nodded dismissively and pointed at Gretchen's elbow. "What's wrong with it?"

"A sprain. But your dad doesn't know a thing about treating one. He's in the other room making some kind of *soup*, when all I really need is a cold compress."

"He's not a normal doctor. He's holistic. Anyway—"

"So what's this Agreement thing?"

Lee looked at Gretchen as though she'd spoken at a register far too high for him to hear. "I don't know what you're—"

"Yes, you do. I'm smart, Lee Vickery. I see things. You can't fool me. Whatever this Agreement is, it means you can't see your dad, doesn't it? You can't even set foot in your dad's side of the house. Which probably means *Felix* can't visit *your* side of the house. Is that it?"

Lee looked like he was going to be sick, but said nothing.

"Fine," Gretchen huffed. "All I was gonna do was offer to help you with *your* problem, because clearly you don't like this Agreement and you can't handle it yourself. I could've told you stuff about the Shades. Stuff only summoners know. I could've even shown you the Book of Rites. But fine, I'll go. *For good.*"

Gretchen pushed past Lee and flung open the conservatory door, clomping down the stairs. Maybe she'd gone too far this time. Bringing up the Agreement—the thing the Vickery brothers were so obviously not supposed to talk about—had seemed like a smart idea. Bait that Lee would bite. But it might have been a stupid approach after all.

And Gretchen certainly hadn't meant to say anything about the Book of Rites. The words had simply come tumbling out, before she could catch and shove them back inside her, where they belonged. So maybe, after all, it was better to leave and come up with another—

"Gretchen, wait! Wait, *wait!*"

Gretchen had forgotten how fast Lee was. He'd caught up with her before the third "wait."

"Hang on," he puffed, rounding in front of her. "You'd show me the Book of Rites?"

Gretchen winced inwardly, but said, "Sure."

Lee's eyes got round. "Isn't that top secret?"

"Well, I'm a Whipple. Duh. So I know how to get hold of it."

Gretchen was fairly certain this was a lie, but she wasn't *absolutely* certain. She knew where the Book of Rites was, but the getting hold of it was trickier. Only her father had that key.

"But—" sputtered Lee. "Aren't there rules against me seeing it?"

Gretchen shrugged. "What my family doesn't know won't hurt them."

"I guess not." Lee lowered his voice to a whisper, as though they were not in a deserted wood but a crowded room, and in danger of being overheard. "Is that true? Do you really know things about the Shades?"

"Sure," said Gretchen, blushing but not knowing why. "And I know a whole lot about Rites. Do you?"

Lee shook his head.

"*See*," said Gretchen. "I know all kinds of things. And I could share them with you. If you help me in return, that is."

"So . . . you want to make a deal."

Gretchen frowned. "I'd call it quid pro quo. You do something for me, I'll do something for you."

"The Rites," Lee said. "Do you think there's one that could break the Agreement?"

Gretchen decided she should be at least a little honest. "I don't know," she confessed. "Especially since I don't know exactly what your stupid Agreement *is*. But . . . we could find out."

"If I help you." Lee was quiet. He looked over his shoulder, again as though someone might be listening in. He was quiet a while longer. Finally, he said, "I'll do it."

Gretchen raised her eyebrows. "You will?"

"Yeah."

"Even though I'm a Whipple?"

"Don't make me take it back."

At last, Gretchen let herself believe him. A grin stretched wide across her face. "That's a promise, Lee Vickery. Understand? You've just made me a *promise*."

"Fine. But that means you've made me a promise, too. I get to see the Book of Rites."

"Sure," said Gretchen. "That's what I said."

Now there was only the small matter of turning her fairly-certain-lie into reality. But Gretchen could worry about that later.

"Hey! *Hey!* Lee, what is she doing?"

Gretchen sighed. For once, things had been going perfectly, so of course Felix *would* ruin it. He was running out to join them, and Gretchen noted with satisfaction that he was much slower than Lee.

"I was just leaving," she said. "And Lee has finally . . . rightly . . . *wisely* agreed to help me. So everything is dandy, thanks."

"You forgot your medicine." Felix held out a bowl filled with murky brown liquid.

Gretchen stared at the broth in disgust. There were crumbled-up bits of plant floating on the surface. She made a teeny retching sound and waved the bowl away. "Keep your magic potion. My elbow doesn't even hurt that much."

"Could've fooled me earlier, calling for a preacher," said Felix, smirking.

"Meet me Monday after school," Gretchen told Lee, ignoring Felix entirely. "On the home-side bleachers of the rec field."

"The home-side bleachers. Got it."

"What's going on?" asked Felix.

Gretchen was pleased by how upset he looked. "None of your business," she said cordially. "See you then, Lee."

Gretchen wouldn't get lost this time. She'd paid close attention to her surroundings, and it would be easier to remember the way back the second time around. She would be home before lunch, and if Gram asked about her elbow, she'd say she hurt it practicing softball.

Now, everything was definitely going according to plan.

It was a half-hour walk back to Avenue B, so Gretchen had plenty of thinking time, and plenty to think over. It was bad enough blurting out anything about the Book of Rites, but now she'd as good as promised Lee access to the book. Could she really help him break whatever strange Agreement ruled the house in Poplar Wood? And what exactly *was* the Agreement?

She might have guessed some of it, but she suspected it was more than just a spell over the house. And who had ever heard of that—a house divided in two?

Gretchen thought back to what had happened in the conservatory. Neither brother had been close enough to push her down the steps, and she certainly hadn't lost her balance; Gretchen had excellent posture and equilibrium—Gram Whipple had made sure of that. Gretchen had been pushed. She'd felt the cold pressure on her shoulders just before she teetered and fell.

"Is that what a Shade feels like?" Gretchen said aloud. "They said Death didn't want me there. Was it . . . *Death* who pushed me?"

Gretchen didn't like this conclusion at all. She would much rather have imagined she'd been pushed by an invisible vampire, or even the vengeful ghost of an ax murderer. To be pushed by *Death himself* . . .

"But it's the only rational explanation," Gretchen said to leafless trees. "Though I don't know if 'rational' is the best word for it. I'm sure most rational people don't believe in Shades, considering they can't see them. Still, if it was Death, then he's a badly behaved Shade. He's supposed to be taking lives at their appointed time, not pushing people down stairs. So if that was Death, he isn't acting right, and Essie Hasting is dead, and Dad said Death killed her . . . something's wrong about this whole thing."

The trees did not reply.

"Or maybe I'm overthinking it."

Gretchen kept walking for some time. Minutes passed, then more minutes still, and the trees began to thin. Just as sounds of distant traffic reached her ears, Gretchen caught sight of something up ahead, standing directly in her path. She slowed to a stop and squinted.

A fox.

A solitary fox, small and suave. Its ears were perked like twin mountain peaks, and its fur was gray and speckled. Gretchen took a few steps closer, but the fox didn't move. It was staring straight at her with bright yellow eyes.

"Hey there, little guy," Gretchen said, taking one step closer, and another.

The gray fox vanished.

It didn't scamper away. It simply *disappeared*, as though it had been nothing but the beam of a flashlight, now switched off. Gretchen rubbed at her eyes and came to the place where the fox had stood. She toed the moldering leaves, and there, underfoot, was a small, perfectly round piece of coal. She scooped it up.

"I thought you were a fox," she said to the coal, feeling stupid. "I *swear* you were a fox a minute ago."

But of course, she received no reply, and without thinking through what she would do with such a souvenir, Gretchen slipped the coal into her coat pocket and walked on.

15

LEE

LEE SAT ON the highest row of the home-side bleachers. It was misting on the field, wet enough to turn the bleachers slick but not so hard that Lee felt he had a right to use an umbrella. Instead, he'd pulled snug the toggles of his jacket hood, crossed his arms over his knees, and waited for Gretchen, who was late.

It had been on a day much like this one—gray and wet—that he and Felix had tried to break the Agreement. Nearly two years had passed since then. Two years for Lee to grow taller and ganglier, and a little wiser, too. He saw now how silly an attempt it had been. How could two eleven-year-old boys have possibly outsmarted *Shades*? Shades! Who were immortal and powerful and not human at all. Shades! Who could change the workings of your mind and the beatings of your heart.

Still, Lee had convinced Felix to run away with him into Poplar Wood and remain hidden there until Death and Memory read their note:

Break the Agreement, or you never see us again.

That year, in sixth-grade history, Lee's teacher had taught the class about *leverage*. Leverage, said Mr. Babbitt, was something in your favor. Something you could offer or withhold, to get what you wanted. For instance, the American colonists' leverage against King George and parliament was their buying power. If they didn't buy the tea and stamps and other highly taxed items the British sent their way, then King George would have to listen to their grievances, so that they would buy things again and he would get his money.

At the time, Lee thought this was a brilliant idea. He and Felix had leverage, after all. They'd lived their whole lives with Death and Memory, training to take over their parents' practice. It was difficult work to find new apprentices. Death and Memory both knew this, and one way or other they meant to get the Vickery brothers to sign their own contracts. But Death and Memory would have no chance of apprentices if Felix and Lee *ran away*. Their very *existence* was leverage.

What Lee did not take into account was that King George did not listen to the grievances of the American colonists. He sent his troops instead.

Lee and Felix had only been able to make it two days in the wood, in their makeshift tent, before a cold front blew in, and they were shaking from chill and hungry for cooked food and frightened by the wolfish howls in the wood. They trudged back to Poplar House, hoping their disappearance had at least shaken the Shades.

The only ones shaken were Vince and Judith Vickery. Nothing else had changed. Death and Memory were unaffected and the Agreement remained as much in place as ever. Worse yet, there was punishment in store for the boys. Lee still shuddered when he thought of his time at Forgetful Pond—a moonless night, alone with dozens of memories, most of them Bad Things and all of them unwanted. And Felix, as with everything about his situation, had it far worse. Death locked him in the cellar, with no food or water, for a full day and night—alone, with nothing but Death's burning candles for company.

Leverage, Lee had decided, was the stupidest concept there ever was, and it belonged only in a history classroom.

And yet.

Though Lee did not speak of the Agreement, he thought of it all the time. He considered it as he lay awake in bed, listening as Memory moved through the house, humming her sad and wordless songs. Once Lee refused his contract, he might live a life as a track star, burning up the Olympics, or as a famous writer or a high school teacher or a dad to fifteen kids, but he would never see his father, and his parents would never again see each other. That was simply the way it had to be.

And yet.

From the time he was little, Lee had known about the Whipples. *Self-serving*, his mother called them. *Without principle.* Summoners were opportunists who used the Shades for personal gain. They saw Death and Memory and Passion as powers to be shackled and bent to human will, rather than beings that humans could learn from and work with. And the summoners, from their high social standing and ivory towers, looked down on the common apprentices and treated *them* like the unworthy ones. All this, Lee knew.

And yet.

He wondered at times, in the dead of night, if people like the Whipples *saw* Shades differently, maybe they *knew* Shades differently. Maybe they knew things he did not.

Lee could not break the Agreement. He had tried before and failed. But maybe there was someone else who could, and maybe that someone was the one person he wasn't supposed to have anything to do with.

Felix hadn't been happy about Lee's deal with Gretchen. He'd spent the better part of an hour that morning trying to convince Lee to back out. In the end, Lee had calmed Felix by telling him that the deal with Gretchen would keep her away from Poplar House. If Gretchen was in town with Lee, then she wouldn't be inclined to instigate any more impromptu acts of vandalism or housekeeping, would she? And then Death wouldn't be inclined to give Gretchen more than just a "warning." Lee shuddered at that thought and tugged extra hard on his toggles.

"This is perfect weather, isn't it?"

Gretchen had arrived. She stomped up the bleachers in bright green galoshes and stopped a few rows down from Lee, where she could fix him with a long, appraising look.

Lee wiped at his running nose. "I don't see why it's so perfect."

"Because we're solving a mystery," Gretchen said with the patience of an adult teaching a kid the ABCs. "Mysteries are solemn affairs. They deserve gray skies and thunder."

Gretchen really was crazy, Lee decided.

"Here's the deal, Vickery," Gretchen said. "You help me, I help you. If everything goes according to plan, I can figure out a Rite to break your Agreement before Christmas. But before any of that, you and I are going on a field trip."

"A field trip where?" Lee eyed the bulky backpack hoisted on Gretchen's shoulder. He had a bad feeling about this.

"Hickory Park."

"Isn't that . . . where they found Essie Hasting's body?"

"Yep."

Lee had a *very* bad feeling about this. "That's a long walk."

"Yes, genius, it is."

Gretchen stomped back down the bleachers, and hesitantly, Lee followed.

"I thought it was still roped off," he said.

"Most of it's open to the general public again. It's just the cliff that's off-limits. They say it's not safe."

"Well, sure, she fell off it."

Gretchen turned suddenly, nearly causing Lee to run into her upturned chin.

"That's what they *say*."

"Uh. Well, what do you think happened?"

"The police, the coroner, the newspaper—everyone who says Essie fell—they all have one thing in common: They report to my dad."

Of course, Lee reflected. Mayor Whipple ran the town. He was rich and powerful, and no one would dare cross his will. It wasn't surprising to hear he controlled the sheriff and the coroner and the *Boone Herald*. But if Lee was understanding Gretchen correctly, that meant—

"You think your *dad* is mixed up in this? That he's got something to do with Essie Hasting?"

"I don't know," said Gretchen. "That's what we're going to find out."

"Okay, but how?"

Gretchen resumed her marching. "You'll see."

"So you have this great big plan that I'm supposed to help out with, and you're not going to tell me what it is."

"Pick up the pace, Vickery, would you? We might have to run at a moment's notice, hide in tight crevices, maybe even punch a few people. You've got to be on your game."

Lee didn't appreciate anyone telling him he was slow. It was not only mean; it was tremendously untrue.

"I don't have to do this, you know," he said angrily. "You could be a little nicer."

"I'm never nice when I'm on a mission. Business supersedes niceness. Memorize that motto, Vickery. Recite it in your sleep. And yes, you do have to do this, if you want to break that Agreement of yours. Quid pro quo, remember?"

Lee wished Gretchen wasn't right.

"That's what we can talk about," Gretchen said.

"Why don't you tell me about your family's little Agreement?"

"*No.*" Lee was surprised by how fast the word came out. Well. Business superseded niceness, didn't it?

"I can't help you break the Agreement if you won't tell me what it is."

"I don't trust you yet. This could be a trick."

"A trick to do what?"

"I dunno, get information from me. To report back to your father."

Gretchen's laugh was loud, with a half dozen snorts thrown in. When the giggles subsided, she said, "You severely overestimate the paternal bond in the Whipple household."

"Still," said Lee. "I don't trust you yet."

Gretchen sighed. "I guess that's fair. I definitely don't trust you."

Lee wanted to say more. He wanted to ask Gretchen exactly what she knew about apprentices, because truth be told, he knew very little about summoners. He'd heard of Rites—the method by which summoners commanded the Shades. His mother had told him they were ancient spells, first created by wicked sorcerers at the dawn of time, but Lee had yet to witness a Rite for himself, and he wondered if his mother might be repeating mere rumors. And sometimes—though Lee would never admit it—he wondered if Rites weren't so very different from the Agreement that ruled his own life, if the Whipples and the Vickeries weren't actually in very similar situations.

There was a lot Lee wanted to ask, but he kept his mouth shut, and neither he nor Gretchen spoke a word the rest of the way to Hickory Park. Gretchen whistled to herself, and she didn't seem to mind the funny looks Lee gave her.

At last, they arrived at the park entrance, and like Gretchen had said, the Do Not Cross tape had been cut down from the trees. Even so, the park was deserted. There were no playing children, no jogging couples, no dogs on walks. Only damp, mulchy earth and tall, bare-branched trees. It was still drizzling, and a low fog poured toward their sneakers.

"Come on," said Gretchen, grabbing Lee by the hand and tugging him along a gravel running trail.

Lee would have felt more uncomfortable about the fact that they were holding hands if Gretchen weren't squeezing his quite so *tightly*. "Ow," he said, wriggling his fingers.

"Don't be a wuss" was Gretchen's reply.

They walked for minutes more until, abruptly, Gretchen left the trail, leading Lee into a tangle of trees. The ground sloped sharply upward, slickened by leaves.

Eventually Gretchen was forced to let go of Lee's hand so that she could better balance her own ascent. They climbed upward and upward, and Lee slipped more than once, conking his shins on roots and rock, his legs a jumbled mess. But finally, the branches cleared, and the mulch turned to crumbling stone and then to . . . nothing at all. They were feet away from a cliff. *The* cliff. Yellow tape strung along the trees made a flimsy, fluttering fence.

Gretchen lifted the tape and motioned for Lee to duck beneath it.

He did not. "You didn't say we were going *here*."

"Where's here?" Gretchen blinked innocently.

"The place . . ." Lee lowered his voice. "The place where she *died*."

"Where else would we be going? If you're running an investigation, the first place you go is the scene of the crime."

Lee narrowed his eyes. "No one's calling it a crime but you."

"C'mon, Vickery. You doing this or not?"

Lee wavered. He thought of the Agreement. He thought of what it'd be like to see his father cheering him on at one of his races. He thought of what it'd be like to eat his mother's cheese biscuits at one supper table, as a whole, unbroken family.

He ducked under the tape.

"Excellent," said Gretchen, and then unzipped her backpack. From it, she removed two flashlights. She handed one to Lee.

"What's this for?" he asked.

"Investigating, of course. We don't have the sun on our side today, so we've got to be extra perceptive. I'm starting on the left edge of the cliff, over there. You start on the right, there. Anything that looks out of the ordinary, holler to me."

Lee made a face, but Gretchen was already marching to her side of the cliff with great purpose. The rain was beginning to pick up. Gretchen could say what she wanted, but Lee happened to think this was the worst possible weather in which to be walking along a deadly cliff. He kept his steps at a decidedly safe distance from the cliff's edge, and he noted that Gretchen did, too.

His flashlight beam revealed little more than rain-laden grass. There were no footprints, and Lee could not say anything was out of the ordinary because he didn't know what ordinary was to begin with. After many minutes of swinging the flashlight and uncovering nothing, he looked to Gretchen, who was now standing closer to the edge of the cliff. He wanted to shout at her to step away, it was dangerous, but he was afraid that shouting suddenly might be more dangerous still.

Gretchen was shining her flashlight at an object on the ground, which she knelt to pick up. Lee hurried to her side. The object was a lined notebook, its pages covered in a tiny scrawl. The paper was turning pulpy in the rain, but the ink did not bleed. He made out words at the top of the page: *Wishing Rite*.

Rite.

Lee opened his mouth, making a sound like a *pop*.

Gretchen started, swinging her light straight into Lee's eyes. "What the heck, Vickery? Try not to be a creep, huh?"

She closed the book and rose to her feet, shuffling several steps away from the cliff's edge.

"What is that?" Lee asked.

"I don't know. I mean, it looks like . . . I don't know."

Gretchen was frowning, the fringes of her dark, damp hair pressed to her cheeks. She tucked her flashlight under her arm and opened the book again.

"Here." She motioned to Lee. "Shine your light."

Lee did, and Gretchen tilted the book for them both to see. Slowly, she turned the pages. Each was covered in black ink—some words only scribbles Lee could not make out. Others were more legible, like the heading he'd seen earlier: *Wishing Rite*. Gretchen flipped to similar headings: *Long Memory Rite* and *Second Chance Rite* and *Guilt Rite*. Beneath each of these headings were lists that looked like recipe ingredients, and beneath the lists were words that were printed clearly, and never running more than six lines long. They reminded Lee of something.

Poetry.

They looked like poems.

There was nothing after *Guilt Rite*. Gretchen flipped and flipped, but only blank pages remained.

"Those can't be . . . *real*, can they?" Lee asked.

"Of course they aren't. Only summoners know Rites. We're the only ones who have the Book of Rites, for crying out loud. This is just . . . I mean, it's just . . . creative writing."

Gretchen had sounded so sure at first, but now it was clear: She didn't know what they were looking at any more than Lee did.

"Do you think that was Essie's?" Lee wasn't sure why he was whispering.

"I don't know," Gretchen whispered back.

She touched the last page with writing on it, titled *Guilt Rite*. Lee read part of the poem:

Your bad deeds will find you like dawn eating night,
Your nightmares will torment your sleep.

Thunder rumbled, low and loud, shaking Lee's ribcage. Gretchen was saying something. *She was reading the poem aloud.*

Maybe it was the rain and the thunder, or maybe it was only the nervous pattering of his heart, but Lee was certain that reciting this poem was *not* a good idea.

"I think you should stop that!" he shouted over the storm.

Gretchen did not stop.

"*Your murder will track you,*" she read on, "*a wrong seeking right.*"

The rain turned harder, pinging into Lee's skin like sharp pellets. He clicked off his flashlight, but it was too late. Gretchen had already seen the last line and was now bellowing it into the storm:

"*Your image will come from the—!*"

Deep. That, Lee knew, was the remaining word of the poem. Only Gretchen never spoke it. Before she could finish the poem, three things happened, all at once.

There was a great clap of thunder.

The ground moved beneath Lee's sneakers.

And Gretchen screamed.

Lee found himself falling backward, and rain was suddenly pounding against his eyelids and up his nose. It took him several seconds to sit up and wipe his face free of water. When he had, Gretchen was nowhere to be seen.

Then—

"Lee!" shrieked an echoing voice. "LEE, HELP!"

It came from his feet. From the edge of the cliff.

Lee crawled toward Gretchen's voice. Bits of stone crumbled beneath the heels of his hands and dropped over the cliff's edge. The fog was so thick that Lee could not make out the ravine below. He did not *want* to see it; he felt woozy enough as it was. And he couldn't be woozy. Gretchen Whipple was in trouble.

The cliff, it turned out, was not a straight drop. The earth sloped dramatically first, turning rocky and jagged before dropping off entirely. It was onto this slope that Gretchen had fallen and was now attempting to climb with no success. Her feet dangled off the cliff's true edge, attempting to find purchase, slipping, and sending down sprays of loose rock.

"Hang on!" Lee shouted, leaning closer to the edge.

Gretchen threw up a hand, and he grabbed her by the wrist.

"*Ow!*" Gretchen shrieked. "You're going to pull my hand off!"

"Give me your other one!"

But Gretchen's other hand was still holding the notebook. She made no attempt to move it.

"*Gretchen!*" Lee shouted. "Let go of the book!"

"NEVER."

"You've got to!"

"NO."

Lee grunted, trying to keep both hands tight around Gretchen's wrist. Then, heaving himself closer to the edge, he shifted his grip down her arm. This way, at least, he wouldn't break her wrist. He tugged, and Gretchen screamed. It wasn't enough to pull her to safety.

"You have to give me both your hands! If you throw the book up here, maybe I can—"

"NO."

For just a moment, Lee lost focus. He looked beyond Gretchen, toward the misty ravine, and his vision began to blotch in big blooming spots of white. He shut his eyes and lunged, trying to grab Gretchen's other arm. Rock moved beneath him, sifting and spilling until he too was hurtling forward, over the edge.

A thought flashed in Lee's brain: Perhaps today was his day. At this very moment, in the cellar of Poplar House, his candle could be fizzling out.

But just as he slid off into the cold, wet void, someone grabbed him by the feet.

"Hang on, Lee!" shouted a voice. "We've got you!"

It was Felix.

16
FELIX

FELIX HAD FOLLOWED them at a distance.

It was the first time he had ever ventured into town on a day that was not Halloween. That morning, his father had two appointments, and Felix knew his presence would be missed. Vince would be angry, and Death would be angrier still. But Felix was far more worried about Lee and what sort of trouble the mayor's daughter had in store for him. Despite all Lee's protests that he would be fine, Felix didn't trust Gretchen Whipple.

As it turned out, he'd been right not to.

When, from the shelter of a dripping tree, he watched Gretchen tumble headfirst off the cliff, he'd run to help. But someone else had gotten there first, and it was that someone who grabbed Lee by the ankles and held on tight while Felix screamed down to his brother.

"Get out of the way, kid," growled the tall, muscled someone. He knocked at Felix with his elbow and gave one mighty heave. He lunged, catching Lee around the waist, and hauled him and Gretchen up onto the muddy ground. Gretchen's eyes were sealed shut, and she was hugging a small, tattered notebook. She stayed that way for many seconds—enough time for the someone to get to his feet and wipe at the wet mud on his jacket.

Gretchen blinked open her eyes. "Th-thank you," she sputtered to the someone. "Thank you so—*Asa?*"

Now they were side by side, Felix saw it: Asa and Gretchen Whipple looked very much alike. Same dark eyes, dark hair, same too-red lips.

With those dark eyes, Asa was staring coldly at his sister. "What are you doing out here?"

"I could ask you the same thing." Gretchen said, scrambling to her feet. "Were you spying on me?" She turned on Felix. "Were *you* spying on me?"

"I don't trust you," Felix said.

"Did—did Dad let you go?" Lee panted at Felix.

"No." Felix felt a stab of dread at the reminder. "But you wouldn't listen to me, and I was afraid she would get you into trouble. And considering you just about *died*, I was right to—"

"Guh, you creeps!" shouted Gretchen. "Don't you know it's rude to follow people?"

Asa shrugged. "I saw you heading to Hickory Park and figured you were up to no good. I was *concerned*."

"Yeah, sure. Don't ever follow me again. You either, Felix. If you wanted to be part of this you should've treated me nicer when you had the chance."

"Why would I want to be part of this?" Felix asked, horrified.

"Oh—oh—whatever!" Gretchen waved him off like he was a bad scent.

"So let's see it then," said Asa. "What was worth dying over, Gretch?"

He grabbed at the notebook his sister was holding, and with one powerful wrench, pulled it free.

"HEY! Give it back!"

The thunder had stilled and the rain had turned back to drizzle, so it was quiet as the three of them watched Asa, waiting to see what he would do with the strange book in his hands.

All the lines in Asa's face turned hard and deep as he opened the book and flipped over its pages. "Where did you find this?" he asked Gretchen.

"Under the rocks." She pointed to the cliff. "It

was hidden, just a corner peeking out. Probably why the police didn't see it before. I *knew* they would miss something. So it's mine, by rights. I investigated. I found it here."

Asa considered the book for a moment more. He pulled out an object from his leather jacket: a lighter. In an instant, he set the notebook alight. Then, in one swift heave, he threw the burning notebook off the cliff, into the fog.

"NO!" Gretchen screamed. "What are you—why would you do that?!"

Asa produced a smile. It looked terrible on him.

"It wasn't yours," he said, pulling out a cigarette to accompany his lighter. As he did, Felix noticed a scar, red and ugly, on his right hand.

"I can't believe you," said Gretchen. "I can't believe—it was *mine*. I found it. And you're just—you're—"

"Don't burst a blood vessel." Asa blew a cloud of smoke in her face. "Why'd that stupid thing matter to you, anyway?"

"It's nothing." Gretchen turned to Lee. "Don't tell him anything!"

Asa cocked his head toward Lee. "This is too good. Hanging with the enemy. It's straight out of *Romeo and Juliet*."

"You don't know what you're talking about," said Gretchen.

"Don't I?" Asa pointed at Lee with his cigarette. "I wonder, Gretch, have you told Gram about your new boyfriend? A *Vickery*?"

"Asa," Gretchen whispered, "don't you dare."

"Oh! I don't dare anything. Just asking questions. My own investigation. Because that's what's going on here, right? My little sister as Sherlock Holmes, trying to uncover who pushed Essie Hasting off a cliff."

Gretchen stuck out her jaw. She looked scared, Felix thought, but was trying not to show it. "We both know who killed Essie," she said. "You hear things, same as I do. You know it was Death."

Felix started. There were two ways to speak about death. The first was universal—patients spoke of death as an event, something impersonal that simply *happened*, the same as skinning your knee or falling asleep. But there was another way to speak of death: as Death, with a capital *D*. Death the person. Death the *Shade*. Death, the most powerful force in Boone Ridge. That was how Gretchen Whipple spoke now.

Asa, however, looked unmoved. In a flat voice, he said, "Everyone dies."

"You know that's not what I mean," snapped Gretchen. "Something happened here. Something people in this town are covering up. And you just threw the one clue I had *off a cliff*!"

"Didn't realize you were such a conspiracy theorist," said Asa. "What were you doing, reading that Rite aloud? Trying to impress a certain someone? Does Romeo even know you're not allowed to summon?"

Lee was breathing hard. He looked at Gretchen with parted lips and chattering teeth. "Y-you can't do Rites?"

Gretchen gave Asa a withering look. "I *might* be able to, if I ever got the chance. It's just a stupid, old rule. Who says secondborns can't summon? I've got the same blood as you."

Asa laughed. "Is that what you think? That you're Gretchen, the summoning prodigy?"

"Why not!" Gretchen shouted. "And I was going to find out for myself, only now you've ruined everything!"

As brother and sister fought, Felix drew near Lee, stepping closer until they were side by side. "Let's get out of here," he whispered.

He put a hand on his brother's shoulder, and Lee met his gaze, and for that moment, Felix thought things might be all right. They could run away and forget all this, be rid of Gretchen Whipple for good. But then something caught Felix's otherwise unseeing eye. Something behind Lee, in the wood.

There was a man standing there—a tall, thin figure between tall, thin trees, dressed in a top hat and a three-piece suit.

It was Death. Death with a capital *D*.

17

GRETCHEN

"WHAT'S THE MATTER with him?"

Gretchen could've gone on fighting Asa for hours. She could've yelled at him for following her, for talking down to her, for making her look bad in front of Lee. There was a whole list of things to scream about. But even in the midst of a shouting match, she could tell something was wrong with Felix. His face had turned a sickly pale, and he was staring hard at the trees—so hard that Gretchen and even Asa turned to see what had caught his attention.

"What's wrong with him?" Gretchen asked again. "What's he looking at?" She couldn't make out anything but bare branches.

"Get him to quit it," Asa told Lee, grinning. "He's scaring my poor baby sister."

"He's not—!" Gretchen caught herself and turned to Lee. "He looks like he's about to croak."

Lee tugged the sleeve of his brother's jacket. "Felix? What is it?"

Felix shuddered. He put both hands to his face. Then, slowly, he lowered the eyepatch that had been knocked out of place in all the commotion. He positioned it back where it belonged, over his right eye.

He breathed in once, deeply. He breathed out.

"I thought I saw . . ." He looked at the trees once more and shook his head. "Nothing. It's nothing."

Everyone remained quiet.

"Well, okay," Gretchen said at last. "That was weird."

Asa was looking at Felix, but not with the usual mean, bully stare. He looked thoughtful, as though Felix were a motorbike he was appraising.

"Where'd you come from?" Asa asked.

Gretchen could've blurted out who Felix was. She wanted to, really. A defiant *I'm hanging out with two Vickeries, so there.* But something told her the brothers might never speak to her again if she spilled those beans.

"It's none of your business," she told Asa.

"Really? Seems a lot like the *family* business to me."

"It's not—that isn't—" Gretchen turned red and silent. There was no point in lying to Asa now. "It's still not *your* business. Next time—ow."

Asa had grabbed hold of Gretchen's shoulder. His fingers dug in hard, and he glared at her with dark, dark eyes. "There won't be a next time, got that? I see you hanging around this park again, I won't keep my mouth shut about what you're doing or who you're with. God knows what Gram would say if she knew what you were up to."

Gretchen wrenched out of Asa's grip. "Why does it matter what I do? You don't care about anyone but yourself."

"I won't say it again. Keep your nose out of this. Rites aren't for kids."

"Yeah, well, I'm not a kid."

Asa shook his head. He laughed a little, all wrongly. "Fine. But if you go careening to your death again, don't expect a helping hand."

With that, her brother stalked away toward the wooded slope, tearing down a long stretch of yellow tape as he went. Moments later, the rev of a motorbike engine ripped through the park.

Reluctantly, Gretchen turned to Lee and Felix. She wished they hadn't heard any of that. Asa had made her look weak. Small. Insignificant.

"I'm sorry I almost got you killed," she muttered to Lee. "I guess now we'll have to try Plan B, which is—"

"Whoa, whoa, whoa!" Felix cried. "Plan B? Are you crazy?! Your brother just said—"

"Asa isn't the boss of me! And neither are you, Felix Vickery. I'll do what I want, and Lee will, too. Won't you, Lee?"

Lee looked uncomfortably between Gretchen and Felix.

"We made a deal, Vickery."

"Um," Lee said.

"Oh." Gretchen crossed her arms. "I get it. You're turning coward on me."

A look crossed Lee's face that Gretchen had not seen there before. She had made him angry.

"I'm not a coward," he said. "And you're a liar! You said you could break the Agreement with a Rite, but Asa just said you're not allowed. When were you going to tell me that? Maybe the same time you told me your top-secret master plan?"

Gretchen wobbled, off-balance. She hadn't thought Lee had this much force in him.

"I—I told you," she stammered, "it's a stupid rule, *antiquated*. It says only the firstborn Whipple is allowed to perform Rites. But it isn't fair that I can't try, just because of when I was born. I'm a Whipple, same as

Asa or my dad. I *could* summon. I just don't know yet, because I haven't done any Rites."

Lee shook his head. "But maybe you *can't* summon. Which means maybe you can't do anything for us. What kind of quid pro quo is *that*?"

"I'm telling you, I think I can! I only need a Rite to prove it, and in case you didn't notice, those just got thrown off a cliff."

"So? Your family has a whole book of them, remember? Why don't you try one of those?"

Gretchen hesitated. It was a mistake.

"You don't really have the Book of Rites either, do you?" Lee cried. "You've made all of this up!"

"I haven't!" Gretchen shouted back. "It isn't made up, I swear! I may have just . . . fudged the details, but I have a plan for everything, including breaking your Agreement."

"So what is it?!" Lee demanded. "You want my help? Then I've got to know the plan. I'm not just going to go running through woods and falling off cliffs when I don't even know what I'm running and falling for."

Maybe Lee had a point, Gretchen reflected. She had been so excited when she'd seen him on those bleachers— when she'd realized Lee Vickery had actually shown up—she hadn't taken the time to consider how much Lee should know.

How much could she really tell him?

Gretchen pointed to Felix. "I'm not saying anything with *him* around."

"No," said Lee, folding his arms. "Felix joins us. You're the one who lied, so you don't get to make the rules anymore, I do. And I say you don't get my help if Felix can't join, too."

Felix looked just as disgusted as Gretchen felt about this sudden proposal. "I don't want to join," he said. "This whole thing is crazy."

"But the Rites," Lee said. "There might be a way to—"

"No. We tried, Lee. We can't. Especially not with *her*." Felix looked accusingly at Gretchen. "What if you can't do the Rites after all?"

Gretchen looked at her galoshes. "I'll figure something out. I—I can ask my father."

"Great," muttered Felix. "Another Whipple."

"Yeah, another Whipple," Gretchen snapped. "In case you aren't aware, we're the only ones who can do Rites, so maybe be nicer, huh?"

"Both of you cut it out," said Lee. He nodded to Gretchen. "You investigated, and I helped. In fact, I almost got killed for you. So now it's time for you to tell me about summoning."

Gretchen coughed. "I don't—"

"Quid pro quo, remember?"

She closed her eyes and sighed. Quid pro quo.

Gretchen wondered, was she about to do something unforgivable? If she told the Vickeries her family's secrets, did that make her a traitor? She hadn't considered that when she'd first made her deal with Lee.

"If I tell you," she said, "it has to be under the strictest confidence."

Lee nodded solemnly. "Of course."

"All right." Gretchen shouldered her backpack, her mind made up. "We'll go to my place. Gram will be at bridge club, so we'll have the house to ourselves until six. Is *he* going to come?" She pointed to Felix.

"I don't know." Lee turned to his brother. "Are you?"

Felix looked pained, as though someone were pinching him very hard. But he nodded.

"Then I guess I can't stop you," sighed Gretchen. "Come on, both of you."

18
LEE

Lee couldn't stop his hands from shaking, even after Gretchen had lit a fire in the library hearth. His clothes were damp and his skin chilled, but Lee suspected the shakes weren't entirely owing to the rain. He could still feel Gretchen's arm slipping through his hands, still see the fog-shrouded ravine and the very great distance between him and it. Today, he had almost died.

He was upset that Felix had followed him—had left home without permission—and Lee feared what punishment awaited his brother. To take his mind off that unpleasant thought, he looked around the wood-paneled library, at its rows and rows of books, stacked and fitted all about him.

Gretchen stood atop a tall stepladder and was scanning a row of books five shelves up. She ran her finger along the spines, a soft *tip-tip-tip*. Then the *tip-tip*ping stopped, and Gretchen cried out, "Here it is!"

She pulled out a book and clutched it one-armed as she hopped off the ladder and settled on the sofa next to Lee. Felix, who had said nothing since their departure from Hickory Park, sat across from them on an ottoman near the crackling fire.

"What is it?" Lee asked, scooting closer to Gretchen and looking the book over. The cover was deep green and resembled snakeskin. Or maybe it really *was* snakeskin.

Gretchen opened the book, and a strong scent of must emerged from the pages.

"Ugh," said Lee.

"I know," said Gretchen. "Like something died."

Felix snorted. "That isn't what death smells like."

"Why thank you, Mr. Expert," said Gretchen. Clearly, she and Felix meant to argue every point on principle.

"This is the best book on the topic of summoning," Gretchen said. "It was made by the very first mayor of Boone Ridge, over two hundred years ago."

She tapped the first page of the unnamed book, on which there was an ink drawing of a coiled snake. Its head was lifted ever so slightly, and its slit eyes stared up at Lee in a way that sent him shaking once more.

"This is how I learned most of what I know, really." Gretchen turned the page. "It's so clear. Everything is arranged all nice and neat. A chapter on Memory. A chapter on Death. A chapter on Passion. A chapter on 'practical applications.' There are lots of pictures and charts. It's very comprehensive."

Lee took a good look at the table of contents. Memory, Death, Passion. Never had Lee seen their names written out like this, in one place—a testament to their reality. Of course *he* knew they were real, but no one in town or at school ever spoke like they were.

"Humans are content to live small lives," Lee's mother had told him once. "They know greater forces are at work, but it's such a lot of effort to see or understand them. It's easier to just eat your breakfast and watch your favorite television shows."

But then, Lee thought, Gretchen wasn't an ordinary human. And she certainly hadn't been raised to live a small life. She saw what Lee saw, and she understood, but in a different way than he ever had.

"What sort of pictures?" asked Felix, scooting the ottoman closer.

Gretchen flopped the pages over to the center of the binding. There were two drawings, each covering a full page. One was captioned *Death Rite*, the other *Memory Rite*. Felix let out a shout.

"What?" said Lee, growing excited. "Is that what they look like, then?"

The pictures were ink drawings. In one, Death stood tall, a young man dressed in an expensive-looking suit; he held a top hat in one hand and a pair of metal pincers in the other. Under his gaze, a small girl was kneeling with tears in her eyes, bent over the figure of a lifeless old man.

In the other picture, labeled *Memory Rite*, a sharp-jawed woman, dressed in lace from throat to ankle, stood over a boy, who sat cross-legged with a large book titled *Book of Rites* in his lap.

Felix had told Lee how Death and Memory appeared to his otherwise sightless eye. He'd described Death as a man in a suit and Memory as a beautiful lady, Queen Anne's lace threaded in her hair. But the pictures in Gretchen's book were more than vague descriptions: they were slopes of noses and turns of cheekbones and curves of ears—clear and unmistakable faces.

"That's them, all right," Felix whispered.

Gretchen laughed in a breathy, nervous way. "So it's true. You do live with them. You can see them."

"I see them every day." Felix tapped his eyepatch. "In this eye."

Gretchen pointed to Lee. "And you hear them through your deaf ear."

Lee nodded.

"They live with you," she said softly. "I thought . . . I thought maybe Dad was lying about that. It can't be easy, can it? Living with *Shades*?"

Lee exchanged a look with Felix. They shouldn't be talking about this, he knew. Not with a Whipple. But then, only a Whipple would understand.

"No," he said. "It's not easy."

"The Agreement."

Gretchen did not say it like a question, but Lee knew it was. He and Felix were still looking at each other. Felix's look said *We can't say more.* Lee's said *We've already said too much.*

"Gretchen," Lee said, "what exactly do you know about apprentices?"

"That you suck," Gretchen said promptly. "The Shades offer you one nice thing, and for that you give them the rest of your lives. And then you don't care about humans anymore, you just do whatever your Shade tells you, like mindless drones."

Lee decided it was not worth pulling apart these words.

"So you know apprenticing is usually hereditary, right?" he asked.

"Sure," said Gretchen. "Like summoners. You grow up with the family business. And then when you're sixteen you choose whether or not to sign an apprenticeship contract."

"Right," said Lee. "That's how it was for our parents. Mom's family has been apprentices since the Great Depression. And Dad's has since . . ." Lee frowned, trying to remember.

"Since 1865," said Felix. "It used to be Carvers, but the last of them died off in the Civil War."

"Right," said Lee. "Felix remembers the dates better than me."

"And they didn't just give away their lives for 'one nice thing,'" Felix said tightly. "They were trapped into signing those contracts. Bad things happened to them, and they had to sign to make the bad things better. They—they didn't really have a choice, they—"

Felix had grown red in the face. He looked liable to explode, and for that reason, Lee cut in. "*Anyway*, Felix lives with our dad and Death, and I live with our mom and Memory."

"Only, you can't see each other," Gretchen said, her eyes bright. "I mean, Felix, you can't see your mom, and Lee, you can't see your dad."

Lee nodded.

"They can't see each other, either," said Felix. "Mom and Dad."

Gretchen frowned. "Is that . . . normal for apprentices?"

The brothers looked uneasily at each other.

"No," said Lee. His mind flooded with the stories his mother had told him—vivid, like they were his own memories.

"Normally," he said, "Shades don't live anywhere near each other. They don't want to know each other's business. They don't associate. Here in Boone Ridge, especially, Death and Memory don't get along. Something happened a while back, and they got into a big fight. And, well, Passion knew that and decided to pull a prank on them. Thought it'd be funny to make their two apprentices fall in love."

Gretchen's eyes got big. "Your mom and dad."

"Yes. And, well, it worked. They fell in love before they knew who the other was, and by then it was too late. They tried to keep it secret for a while."

"But Death and Memory found out," guessed Gretchen.

Lee nodded. "They were, um, *mad*. Death threatened to kill Mom before her time. Memory threatened to remove all memory of Mom from Dad's head. Then Mom found out she was pregnant with me and Felix. So Mom and Dad begged to draw up a new contract."

"The Agreement," said Gretchen.

"Mom and Dad agreed to never see each other again and to each take one son. Mom took me to raise as Memory's new apprentice, and Dad took Felix to raise as Death's. Then Death and Memory put a charm on Poplar House. The cottage is divided, east and west; we can share the porches, but we can't cross each other's thresholds. So I just . . . don't have a dad. And Felix doesn't have a mom. That's the way it's always been."

"And the way it's always going to be," said Felix, glaring sullenly into the fire.

"Unless you break the Agreement." Gretchen's eyes were focused on the open book in her lap.

"We've tried to break it before," said Felix. "But they're Shades, and we're just kids. It's not going to happen."

The words were prickly, offered to Gretchen but thrown at Lee like accusations.

"Maybe not," Lee said, glaring at his brother. "But if anyone could help us, it'd be Gretchen." He turned to her. "You said maybe there's a Rite that could help us."

Gretchen remained quiet. She looked up from the book. Then, she began to laugh.

19
GRETCHEN

IT HAD BEGUN as a terrible sensation—her belly trembling, her chest shaking like a heavy-duty washing machine. But when Gretchen tried to hold the sensation down, she ended up snorting. Then she gave way completely, bursting into laughter.

"I'm sorry," she gasped around giggles. "I know it's not funny. It's just . . . a lot . . . of new . . . information."

Felix was stony-faced. Lee looked like he was coming down with a stomach virus. Neither boy was laughing along.

"You said you could help," Lee said. "I thought you understood."

"I'm sorry," Gretchen repeated, but this time with much more sincerity, her laughter wheezing away. "I do understand, it's just a little hard to take in, is all. I didn't think Shades were so . . ."

"Petty?" suggested Felix.

"*Human.*" When both brothers flinched, Gretchen said quickly, "I know they're not, but . . . I guess I thought they were more, uh, serious. You know, not the type to pull pranks and fight and stuff."

"Not all of them do," said Lee. "I hear some towns have really good Shades. Fair and kind. Chattanooga, for example, and Asheville. But . . . not here in Boone Ridge."

"Sheesh," said Gretchen. "Apprentices definitely have it worse than us."

Felix folded his arms. "Well, what's the deal with Whipples?"

"Yeah!" Lee waved his hand at Gretchen, as though to say *Now give us something to laugh about.*

Gretchen guessed she didn't have a choice. "Here's how I see it," she said. "Shades make deals. That's what they do—look at your Agreement. Memory can preserve your good memory forever, or erase you from other people's minds. Death can give you a longer or shorter life. Passion can soothe or stir your heart. The other thing they do is bestow special gifts—but only if the right person asks, and only if they follow the Rites. And Rites work like recipes. Each Rite requires certain ingredients—maybe a hair, or a bit of sugar. Everyday things. But they're not so everyday when you mix the ingredients and recite the right poem. When you do that, it's a Rite."

"If the right person asks," Felix repeated.

"Well. You know. A Whipple."

"Sure," said Felix. "Because haven't you Whipples run Boone Ridge for ages? How convenient that you're the 'right people.'"

"Genius," said Gretchen, "it's not *convenient*, it's cause and effect. Whipples aren't the right people because they run Boone Ridge. They run Boone Ridge *because they're the right people.* How do you think my great-great-uncle Whipple got elected mayor in the first place?"

Felix shrugged.

"Because," said Gretchen, "he did what all good politicians do: He made deals. He stayed in office so long because he made a deal with Death. He married the richest, prettiest girl in Boone Ridge because he made a deal with Passion. And he's jammed into every history book here in Boone Ridge because he made a deal with Memory. And the Whipples after him? They did the same thing."

"Wow," Felix said coldly. "That's a family history to be proud of."

"I didn't say I was proud of it. It's just simple fact: I'm a Whipple, so I'm a summoner."

"But you're *not*," said Lee. "Technically. You're not allowed to do Rites."

Gretchen grimaced. She'd known the rules since she was a little girl: Asa was her father's firstborn child, so he had been trained in the ways of summoning, and he would be the next mayor of Boone Ridge. As secondborn, Gretchen inherited no right to summon; she was only entitled to her family's name. She was supposed to live an ordinary life—get a good education, maybe even be sent far away from the family business, to boarding school. So close to the extraordinary, yet ordered to be ordinary—that was Gretchen's fate.

She refused to accept it.

"Gretchen," said Lee, shaking her from her thoughts. "That book you found in the park. Were those real Rites inside?"

"I don't know," said Gretchen, honestly. "I've never seen Rites written down outside of, well—"

She pointed behind the brothers, at the glass case containing the Book of Rites. The afternoon sun was pressing into the stained glass, scattering bits of green and gold light onto the pages.

"Is that . . . ?" whispered Lee.

"Yep."

Felix stiffened. "Dad says that book is evil. It's full of dark, ancient spells."

"Ancient, sure," said Gretchen. "Dark, I guess, depending on who uses them, and for what. Summoners are supposed to use them for the town. Say there's a plague in Boone Ridge. Well, then the summoner does a Rite with Death, asking him to spare the townspeople. Or say there was a horrible battle here. A summoner does a Rite with Memory to get rid of the town's most gruesome stories. Or say people are leaving the town for big cities, better jobs. One thing could make them stay: falling in love. And Passion can make that happen."

"But you said Whipples do Rites for themselves," said Felix, flatly.

"Well, sure," said Gretchen. "It's a perk of the job, I guess. But their main job is to intercede for the town. They're on the people's side. And my thinking is, even though you all are apprentices, you're still people. So maybe there's a Rite I could do to intercede for you."

Lee pointed to the lock on the glass box. "And how are we getting past that, exactly?"

Gretchen studied her hands. "Okay, so I don't exactly have access to the Book of Rites. But!" she shouted, as Lee started to protest. "I have a plan to get it."

"And then what?" said Felix. "You cast a Rite—Oh wait, you *can't*."

"You don't *cast* a Rite. I'm not a *witch*."

"But you don't even know if there's a Rite that can break the Agreement," said Felix. "Admit it. You've been lying about all of it, just to get our help."

"I haven't been lying *exactly*."

Felix shook his head. "You don't believe her, do you, Lee?"

Lee didn't say a word.

"This is ridiculous." Felix got to his feet. "Why should we trust you? First, you're a Whipple. Second, you're a liar. Third, you can't break the Agreement. It's impossible, and you shouldn't make Lee think he can, all for your own stupid plan."

"My plan isn't stupid!" Gretchen shouted. "It's about a girl who died for no good reason, and it's about Death. Doesn't that bother you at all? You're his apprentice-in-training. Don't you care if he's doing bad things?"

"He's Death," Felix said coldly. "Bad things are in the job description."

Gretchen gaped at him. "My father's right. You really have sold your souls to them."

Felix glared at her. She glared back.

A sound came from outside the library—the shutting of a door and the echo of heels on hardwood. Gretchen's eyes widened, and she looked at her watch.

Gram Whipple was home early from bridge club. "Oh no," she said. "Oh no, no, no."

"Who's that?" Lee whispered.

"Gram. You have to go, right now. She never lets me have guests over, especially not *Vickeries*."

Gretchen peered into the hallway. She could hear Gram in the kitchen, rummaging.

"Okay. Come on. You're going out the window." She motioned for the boys to follow her into the hallway, but Felix hung back.

"Did you want us to get caught?" he asked. "Is that what this was? A setup?"

"Good Lord," groaned Gretchen. "If it were a setup, I wouldn't be sneaking you out through the window, now would I? I'd just *let you get caught*." She marched across the hallway to the bathroom, making her strides as long and swift as possible. The brothers followed, and Felix shut the door behind them—*loudly*.

"Gretchen?" called Gram Whipple's voice. "Gretchen, is that you?"

Gretchen glared murderously at Felix, even while shouting, "Yup! It's me!"

"Gretchen Marie, how many times have I told you, the guest bathroom is for guests only!"

Gretchen rolled her eyes. Gram Whipple had told her this *many* times. Such reminders usually turned into a long-winded rant, so she let Gram Whipple go right on ranting as she shoved open the bathroom window and waved for Lee to exit. He stepped onto the toilet lid.

". . . rumple up the hand towel, as though it were meant to be used! That towel is *decorative*, child. If you knew the pretty penny I spent—"

"Go, *go*," Gretchen said, as Lee disappeared out the window and Felix climbed on the toilet after him. But just as Felix reached for the window ledge, he gave Gretchen a dirty look, and a split second later, his foot slipped. Felix lost his balance and fell, knocking over a potpourri jar in an almighty clatter.

"GRETCHEN WHIPPLE, WHAT IN GOD'S NAME IS GOING ON IN THERE."

Gram's voice was getting closer, accompanied by clacking heels.

"*Go!*" Gretchen whisper-shouted, helping Felix to his feet and watching, heart aflutter, as he made the climb again—this time successfully. Just as he fell out of sight, she slammed shut the window, and Gram flung open the door.

Gretchen looked sheepishly up at her grandmother. "Oops?" she squeaked.

Gram clenched her jaw. For one long moment, she said nothing. Then she commanded, "You'll clean that up. You will bleach that toilet and clean that sink and sweep and mop that floor. Then you will go straight to your room. Lord knows I don't have time for this, not with the gala coming up."

Only when Gram Whipple had clacked back to the kitchen did Gretchen let out a breath. It had been a close call, but she could accept her punishment. Bleaching, she knew, was better than boarding school.

20
FELIX

ON THE WAY home, Felix's mind was abuzz with far more thoughts than he'd ever imagined could fit inside it.

Rites.

The word stung his insides over and over again, like an angered hornet.

Rites.

Rites.

Rites.

He was thinking, too, of the books in the Whipple library. Tome after tome, stacked high and wide across— so much knowledge contained within their bindings. Words and ideas that Felix had never had access to, all because of his apprenticeship. If there was a Rite that could change all that, could place those books into his hands . . .

"What's going to happen to you?"

Felix started at Lee's soft question. The brothers had walked through town and much of the wood in silence. Now, only minutes from Poplar House, the threat of Felix's punishment hung heavy.

"I guess what happened last time," said Felix. He remembered, with terrible clarity, the damp of the cellar. A shudder rattled up his spine.

"You shouldn't have followed me," Lee said.

"I was worried."

"No, you thought I wasn't smart enough to take care of myself. That I didn't know what I was getting myself into."

"Well you didn't, did you?"

"If I want to go falling off a cliff," said Lee, "then I've got the right."

This was one of the stupidest things Felix had ever heard Lee say. "Don't thank me or anything," he muttered.

"I won't, because you didn't have to come." In a whisper, Lee added, "I just don't want him to hurt you."

What could Felix say to that? Death *would* hurt him, and that was certain from the moment Poplar House came into view. Vince was standing on the front porch, and when Felix raised his eyepatch, he saw Death by his father's side. Felix stopped walking, his feet stuck into the brown, rotting leaves.

"What?" Lee whispered. "Is he there?"

"They both are. It'll be fine, just go inside."

"Felix, I—"

"I don't need your help."

"I won't—"

Felix shoved Lee in the chest, hard.

"Go home. Go. Home."

Lee gritted his teeth and said, "Fine." He stormed across the clearing and up the front steps, slamming himself inside Poplar House's west end. Felix saw his father jump as he looked toward the sound and realized that Lee was near.

You'll never see him, Dad, Felix thought as he trudged to the porch. *You'll never see him and you'll never see Mom again.*

"Felix Jerome Vickery, where in God's name have you been?"

Felix could not look his father in the eye. He could do nothing but stare at Death.

Death's skin and lips were pale as plaster. His eyes were ice blue and his lashes long. His figure was tall, poised perfectly at the shoulders, and his dress was immaculate: always the black suit, bow tie, and top hat.

Felix hated every elegant inch of him.

He was glad, at least, that he could not hear Death's voice. Lee had told him that it was beautiful but frightening, like a lullaby that made you more afraid of the dark. But Felix had felt the full weight of Death's stare. Those blue eyes bore into him with an unforgiving burn—a wordless act of violence.

"Felix."

He at last turned to his father. "I had to leave," Felix told him. "Lee was in trouble."

Vince's eyes shifted and dimmed. Felix was hurting his father, he knew, just by mentioning his brother's name.

"Is he all right?" Vince asked.

Death set his hand on the crook of Vince's elbow. He shook his head, and Felix did not need to hear his voice to know the import of this message. *No,* Death was saying. *You cannot know.*

Vince breathed in once, deeply. "Felix," he said, "you know there are consequences for disobeying the rules. I had two important appointments this morning, and your role in this house is vital to—"

"I know. But Lee was more important."

"It's not your place to decide what is more important."

"No, it's *Death's,*" said Felix. "You wouldn't punish me for helping Lee, Dad. I know you wouldn't. It's Death who's angry. He followed me. He saw where I went. And he's angry about it. Aren't you!" He looked straight at Death. He didn't know why he was pleading. There was no point.

"Death is going to take you to the cellar. Do you understand?"

Felix could hear, beneath those words, a string of unvoiced questions. His father was asking, *Why is Lee in trouble? Why did you disobey again? Why did you bring this punishment on yourself when you know I am powerless to stop Death?*

Death wrapped his cold arm around Felix's shoulders and led him into the house. It was a long way down to the cellar—two full spirals of eleven stairs each that Felix had counted long ago, when he was very young and had first begun to make trips up and down them. Back then, counting stairs had been a much better use of his mind than imagining the dark, dreadful things that could be lurking in the cellar, just out of the candlelight's reach. Felix had grown braver with every year he worked as Death's apprentice-in-training. Now that he was thirteen, the shadows no longer scared him.

What scared him were the candles.

Each thin, red candle was a life, and each flame was a life-breath. When a flame went out, that life was gone forever, and it was Felix's job to fetch the extinguished candle and store it away in one of Death's three wooden trunks. Sometimes, the wax was still warm.

Every so often, Death would haul one of these trunks up the cellar stairs and drag it into the dark of Poplar Wood. When he returned, the trunk was empty, the candles gone. Felix wondered where Death emptied those candles—if it was like Lee's Forgetful Pond, a place of uneasy magic. Whatever the case, the candles were taken away, like the lives they represented. Felix feared those candles, and Death knew it. That was why the cellar was such a very good punishment.

Death stopped on the first landing. Felix stopped with him, but Death shook his head and pointed a bony index finger downward.

It was happening again.

Felix creaked down the remaining stairs. He tried to breathe slowly, to calm the wild *thump* of his heart. He stepped into the flickering light as the cellar door closed above him.

21
GRETCHEN

GRETCHEN KNOCKED ON the bedroom door.

Asa hadn't answered the first time, but Gretchen knew he was in there from the heavy percussion and screeching electric guitars. Any other day, she would've given up after the first knock and let Asa be. But she needed an answer to her question today. She pounded louder, to be heard over the raging music.

Another half minute passed, and still no response. Gretchen raised her fist to knock a final time, but as she did the door swung open, and Asa stood before her. His cheeks were blotchy and damp. It looked like he'd been crying. But that couldn't be. Gretchen decided the red in his face must be from anger.

"What?" Asa barked.

"Uh," said Gretchen. "Got a minute?"

Her brother regarded her with suspicious eyes. This was odd, what Gretchen was asking, and both of them knew it. Gretchen didn't knock on Asa's door, and he did not knock on hers. They didn't talk, not unless Asa had something mean to say.

Gretchen said, "I have a question to ask."

"Forget about it," said Asa, shutting the door.

"No, wait!" Gretchen shoved her foot across the threshold. "Just hear me out, okay? I'm only asking something theoretical."

Asa stilled the door. Maybe to prevent a showdown with Gretchen's sneaker, or maybe because just a tiny part of him wanted to know what she'd say.

"Go, then," he said. "You've got a minute."

"All right." Flustered, Gretchen searched her mind for the story she had rehearsed. "Say there was a summoner who made a deal with a Shade, but it turned out it wasn't a good deal. But then, say that summoner got amnesia! Like, they completely forgot how to do Rites. Could another summoner help them out? I mean, is there a Rite you could do to *undo* the first, bad Rite?"

Asa's gaze darkened with every word Gretchen spoke. When she finished, he was shaking his head.

"What are you talking about? How would that ever happen?"

"I told you, it's hypothetical. *Hypothetically*, is there a Rite that undoes other ones?"

"No," said Asa. "A deal with a Shade is a deal forever. They can't be undone."

"Ever?"

"Never. Rites are permanent. That's why they're dangerous."

"But . . . well, what if there's an undoing Rite we just don't know about?"

Asa threw a hand in the air. "Sure, Gretch, go ahead and think that."

"Well, I don't know what to think! Nobody here gives me answers. Dad shared all his secrets with you, and I don't get to know anything."

"I told you to stay out of it," said Asa.

"But I'm part of this family! I'm a Whipple, too!"

Asa slammed his hand against the doorframe. "Stop talking like that," he growled. "Like we're some special breed. Don't you understand what being a Whipple means? We're *cursed*, and we curse those around us. People get hurt because of us. People—people *die* because of us. That's what it means to be a Whipple. There's nothing special about it."

Gretchen didn't know what to say. She gripped and released the hem of her sweater, blinking against tears.

Asa stepped away from the door, startled, it seemed, by the words that had poured from his mouth. He looked almost . . . sorry.

"You've had your minute," he said, and he shut the door in Gretchen's face.

She kept tugging at her sweater, staring at the TOXIC WASTE SITE sign that hung from Asa's door.

People die because of us, Asa's voice said again, angry and strange.

Gretchen wondered if people really had died because of the Whipples. Because of Rites.

She wondered if Asa was talking about Essie Hasting.

22
LEE

Lee did not see Felix for two full days. Then, Thursday morning, as Lee was leaving for school, he found his brother on the front porch, hanging herbs to dry from the rafters as though nothing had happened. Lee ran to him, but Felix shrugged himself violently out of Lee's embrace.

"I'm fine," he said. "It wasn't a big deal, and I don't want to talk about it."

And that was all he said.

Lee left the house, feeling pushed out, unwanted. He knew Felix had suffered. He wanted to listen to what had happened, to try to make things better. But Felix, it seemed, wanted nothing of the sort. He meant to keep the suffering to himself, locked away in a place Lee could not reach. And so, Lee did not reach again. When he returned home that night, he said nothing to Felix. When Felix wanted to talk, he would.

Only, Felix did not speak that day or the next day, or the next. He did not join his brother on the porch, or in the conservatory. They weren't fighting—no shouts or blows. But Lee wondered if this silence might be worse than any fight. It stretched out, uninterrupted, with no visible end.

Even in the silence, Lee was worried about his brother. He couldn't concentrate for more than half-minutes at a time at school. He didn't run on the track after practice just for fun, as he usually did. He ate his lunch in the supply closet, atop an overturned mop bucket, rather than join the kids at the orange table.

And above all else, he stayed away from Gretchen Whipple.

When he saw her quicken her steps in the school hallway, trying to catch up with him, he ducked into the boys' restroom. When he felt her eyes burning holes into his back in English class, he didn't look her way.

Back on that wet Monday, they had made no future plans. He and Felix had toppled out of the bathroom window, and that had been that. Now, seeing Gretchen made Lee feel acutely uncomfortable. She *knew*. He'd told her secret things about his life and the Agreement, and Gretchen had *laughed* about it. Now Lee felt a horrible sensation every time he saw her, like she'd caught him stripped down to his underwear, and things could never, ever be the same.

The more Lee had thought about it, the more he'd come to realize that *Gretchen* was the one responsible for Felix's punishment. If she hadn't come calling at Poplar House or convinced Lee to make a deal, Felix would never have had to chase after them. And all for what? Gretchen had done nothing for Lee but almost get him thrown off a cliff.

For two weeks, Lee had done an excellent job of avoiding Gretchen. Then, on the Monday before Thanksgiving, his luck ran out. She found him in the supply closet.

"It smells like salami in here" was all she said before closing the door and flipping on the light. "Why the heck are you eating in the dark, Vickery?"

Lee didn't answer. He was eyeing the door, wondering if he could bolt past Gretchen and escape.

"Hey!" Gretchen caught his gaze. "Don't even think about it. You owe me an explanation. Why have you been ignoring me?"

Lee shrugged. He bit into his lukewarm corn dog.

"I told you a lot of really private stuff, Vickery. I let you—the enemy!—into my house. And now you go and give me the cold shoulder, for no reason. I thought . . . I thought you weren't like the rest of those orange-table jerks."

Lee snapped up his chin. "I'm not."

"Oh yeah? We made a deal, and now you won't even look at me. You're embarrassed, huh? You think that Dylan and Emma are going to kick you to the curb if they find out we're friends."

Lee blinked in confusion. "What?"

"Well, that's it, isn't it?" said Gretchen, her voice suddenly unsteady. "I'm not cool enough?"

"*What?* No! It's not that, it's . . ." Lee looked away and in a quieter voice said, "Felix got in trouble for breaking the rules. And I know Death hurt him, only he won't talk about it. He won't talk to me at all. And look, I believe the things you said. I think you might be able to help us. But I'm really worried about Felix right now, so it just hasn't seemed like the right time to go on another investigation."

Gretchen blinked. "You're just . . . worried about Felix?"

Lee nodded.

"Well you could've told me that, you know. I would've backed off."

Lee looked at Gretchen, dubious. "Really?"

"Just because I want your help doesn't mean I *need* it."

Lee sniffed. "You made it sound a lot more dramatic when you were chasing me down."

"Yeah, well, I can be dramatic."

Lee laughed. "Tell me about it." The closet grew quiet, and then Lee said, "It really *does* smell like salami."

"Sorry about your brother," Gretchen said.

"You don't even like him."

"Not really. But you like him, and I like you, and you're sad, so I'm sorry."

Lee looked at Gretchen. "You like me?"

Gretchen looked straight back at him. "Yeah. I *like* you. I know I accused you of cowardice before, but you've proved yourself. I think you're all right, Vickery. Is that going to make things weird?"

Lee stared.

Gretchen smiled. "A girl's never told you that before, has she?"

Lee thought about Emma holding his hand under the orange table. "Not exactly."

"Well, I don't want to *kiss* you or anything," she said, making a face. "I only mean you're not like other kids, and I like that about you."

"Even though I'm a Vickery."

"Sure."

Lee considered this. He considered the fact that his face felt warm. He considered that he was alone in a closet with the mayor's daughter.

"You're not too bad either," he said. "For a Whipple."

"Appreciate it." And though Gretchen smirked like she didn't care, her cheeks were pink. "Anyway, even if you're temporarily bailing on your side of the deal, I'm still upholding mine."

Lee's heartbeat picked up. "You found a Rite to break the Agreement?"

Gretchen grimaced. "Well, not exactly. I've been asking around, but no one's telling me much. Typical. The only thing left to do is go to the source itself. Remember how I said I had a plan to get the Book of Rites?"

Lee nodded.

"So here's the deal: I'm doing this to help you, but I'll need a little help *from* you."

"Do I have to crawl through your bathroom window again?"

"I make no promises."

"Well . . . okay, I guess."

"You free this Wednesday night?"

"Yeah."

"Good. Then come to my place, eight o'clock."

"It'll be dark then," Lee said.

"Uh, yeah. Okay?"

Lee swallowed and nodded. He wasn't about to tell Gretchen that he didn't like walking in Poplar Wood alone at night. She'd decided he wasn't a coward, and he meant to keep it that way.

"Eight o'clock," Gretchen repeated. "Come around to the back of the house. I'll be looking out for you. And hey." She pointed a finger. "I'm still holding you to your end of the deal. Once Felix is better, we're back to figuring out what happened at Hickory Park. Got that?"

"Is your brother going to show up again?"

Gretchen scowled. "Definitely not."

"Then okay," said Lee. "The deal's still on."

Gretchen nodded, businesslike. She reached for the door, then stopped. "And Lee? Maybe this time you shouldn't tell Felix."

Lee thought about his brother. About the way he'd shoved away Lee's hug and stoppered up all his words for days on end. As though he couldn't be bothered with Lee's concern.

"No," he said. "I won't tell Felix a thing."

23
FELIX

THREE CANDLES HAD gone out in the cellar.

It hadn't mattered that Felix had shut his eyes, or that he had gripped his ears and tried to conjure happy memories of summer days he'd spent with Lee. Death wasn't a mere matter of the five senses; Death was beyond them.

It began as a scent. Felix smelled it even with his nose pressed firmly between his knees. Honey and rotten meat commingled—one scent so sweet it made him salivate, the other so rank it tugged a gag from his throat.

Then came the sound of shrieking—shrieks like rusted nails dragged against metal, over and over. Red blotches burst and bled in the dark of Felix's eyelids. Then the color seemed to travel down to his throat and touch the back of his tongue with a taste like curdled milk. Death wrapped around him so completely, colder and damper on his skin than the already cold dampness of the cellar.

There was no safe place when a life was snuffed out. The sensations lasted for hours on end, and then as suddenly as they came on, they left. There were thousands of candles alight in the cellar, but Felix never had trouble finding the one that had been extinguished; that smell of honey and meat remained pungent in the last smoky fizzle. Then, as was Felix's duty, he retrieved the candle and placed it inside one of Death's chests, among all the other dead lives within.

Three times he had done this.

Felix had not begged for mercy or pounded on the cellar door, offering bargains with Death to let him out. He knew that Death never gave second chances. He knew, too, that his father was under Death's command and could not rescue him. So he endured his punishment in silence.

Death unlocked the cellar door at the end of the second day. Sweet, fresh air came pouring down the stairs, nearly drowning Felix in relief. When he emerged, he allowed his father to bundle him in quilts, and he fell asleep with Vince at his bedside.

In the morning, Felix's work resumed as usual, and he refused the hug that Lee offered him. Life carried on for nearly two weeks, during which time Felix made no attempt to talk to his brother, and Lee made no attempt to talk to him.

Then, early on a Monday morning, there was a patient to see Vince. Felix stood silently in the corner of the examination room as his father asked the elderly man to lie down. Felix was nervous for the old man. The older a patient, the more likely it was that Death would take out his iron pincers and extract their life.

As it turned out, that morning's appointment was a fortunate case. Death stood at the head of the table, his shadow falling over the man's bearded cheek. Then Death whispered to Vince the names of the herbs needed to cure the old man's arthritic complaint, and once Felix had concocted the prescribed broth, the old man left Poplar House with a lighter step than the one that had brought him.

The good visit did not mean Felix was in good humor. Questions turned over in his mind, as much in need of answering as they had been a week before: What if Rites really could work? And what if there was a Rite to end the Agreement, once and for all?

Felix knew his place. He had tried to forsake it once, to run away with his brother and break his bonds. They had failed, and that, he thought, had been the end of it.

But three candles had gone out before Felix's left eye. A punishment for a broken rule that should not have existed, an Agreement that ruled his life and would for at least three more long years. An Agreement that would always keep his family apart.

There was a world outside of that Agreement. A world of grand libraries, books, and endless knowledge. A world that Death had never allowed Felix to see, a future of possibilities Felix could not imagine, so limited was the sphere he'd been kept inside. Now Felix felt himself expanding, a great balloon growing larger and larger, pressing at the edges of his small sphere's glass confines.

He was not sure he'd fit inside much longer.

24
LEE

LEE UNWOUND THE violet ribbon from its spool.

A patient had visited Poplar House while he'd been at school, and the volume of the memories left behind was extraordinary for just one person. Three jars sat on the canning table, filled to their brims with a thick, tar-like liquid—all memories of Bad Things. Whoever the patient was, they must've endured terrible tragedy. Lee was glad, at least, that the unfortunate individual had found Judith and was now rid of such foul remembrances.

Bad Things were the most difficult to store. They required the use of the rickety stepladder, and even then Lee had to reach above his head to slide them onto the shelf. Today, the jars were still fresh and unpleasantly hot to the touch.

Lee licked his chapped lips as he finished off his final violet bow. For a moment, he did nothing more than stare at the three jars, all labeled *Forget*. Then he picked up the first of the jars and ascended the ladder. He reached up to the bare space on the fifth shelf, jar in hand, the glass hot against his skin. Then, just as Lee was tipping the jar onto the shelf's edge, it slipped through his curled fingers.

"NO!" Lee cried.

The jar hit the floor with a *crash*.

Lee scrambled down the ladder toward the damage, but it was too late. The black liquid hissed from the fissures of broken glass, and out came a smell like bad eggs. Lee covered his nose and ran for the door, but as he did, his legs grew heavy. Then, suddenly—

He was standing in a school hallway, turning his locker combination with practiced ease: left to 35, right twice to 15, left once to 20. He felt a light pressure on his shoulder and turned, an annoyed remark on the tip of his tongue. Then he saw her face, and the words dissolved.

"Essie," he said. "What do you want?"

The question came out far meaner than he'd intended, and he watched with regret as Essie's face fell from hopefulness to hurt.

"You don't have to be that way with me," she said.

"I didn't mean . . ." He shook his head, then turned back to his locker, shoving his geometry book inside. "Whatever. Why are you even talking to me in public?"

"I don't know. Considering you don't ever acknowledge me."

"It's better that way."

"Then stop complaining." Essie tossed her hair. "I was going to tell you what I found out about the stone, but since your locker is so much more interesting—"

"Wait."

He reached out as she turned from him. His fingertips brushed her elbow, and Essie stiffened. She fixed her eyes on his.

"Just meet me in the park, okay?" he said. "There's no reason to change things now."

Essie shrugged. "No reason at all."

He watched her leave. He wanted to follow, to apologize for always saying the wrong things when other people were around.

Why couldn't Essie understand? At the park, he felt at home. When it was just the two of them, seated on the mossy earth, overlooking the ravine, sharing stories and more—only then could he be himself. Not here. Never here, amidst a swarm of high schoolers who did nothing but taunt and gossip and jostle and—

Lee gasped for air. The vision of the hallway bled away from his eyes, replaced by a cobwebbed ceiling. He was lying on his back, skin wet with cold sweat. The room smelled faintly of blood, and there was a sizzling sound close to his ear. With trembling hands, Lee pushed himself to a sit. Something sharp bit into his left palm, and he looked down to see a shard of glass lodged in his skin, blood peeking from the wound. Beside him lay the shattered canning jar and a circlet of violet ribbon, still neatly tied in its bow.

Lee got to his feet, his ears perked for any sounds from outside the canning room, afraid that Memory or his mother had heard the commotion. But all was silent in the west end of Poplar House. With his uninjured hand, Lee creaked open the door and peered into the hallway. His mother's bedroom door was shut; she was probably resting. He heard no sound of Memory's humming in his left ear; she must've stepped out for a walk through the wood, as she often did on sunlit afternoons.

Lee scrambled to the bathroom, where he washed away the blood from his cut and took a bandage and rubbing alcohol from the medicine cabinet. Once he was patched up, he returned to the storage room and locked the door behind him. He surveyed the damage: only the broken remains of a canning jar, none of its contents.

"Well, of course," Lee whispered. "The memory's in my mind. It's mine now."

When Lee closed his eyes, he could see it all again—relive it as he had when he had been unconscious on the canning room floor, though not quite so vividly as before. He replayed the memory. He played it again. And again. And then, just its beginning.

"*Essie.*"

Whoever's memory he now possessed had known Essie Hasting. Lee had never met Essie in person. He'd seen her picture once, alongside the newspaper headline that announced her death, but this new memory of her barely resembled the lifeless, black-and-white shot. She was bright-eyed and full of color and life.

Lee played the memory through once more, this time skipping hurriedly to its end. There was nothing new there, nothing he'd missed upon his first viewing. It had been a memory of a conversation in a school hallway, and that was all. What was so terrible about that? What had been so foul about this memory to turn it thick and black, worthy of a place on the fifth shelf?

Maybe it's just foul now because she's dead, he thought.

Lee stared at the remaining two glass jars on the canning table. Those memories belonged to the same patient. What were the chances that they, too, were about Essie?

Lee could be clumsy and forgetful. He had broken a memory jar before. But he had never *stolen* one. Now, he was going to steal two. He'd decided as much even before he'd finished sweeping up the shattered remains of the first jar. He settled his plan as he snuck the dustpan's contents out to the wood and buried the glass beneath a pile of red leaves. By the time he returned to the canning room, he had no remaining doubts. He took both jars. The glass was still hot to the touch, but his grip was now firm and unshakable.

Only after Lee had taken the jars to his bedroom and pushed them under his bed, on the side farthest from reach, did he begin to feel terribly sick. His stomach curdled with nausea, and he crawled onto the bed and shut his eyes.

"I should wait, then," he whispered, speaking aloud to push away the tumult in his stomach. "I'll wait until I feel better before I open the next memory. And if it's about Essie, too, I have to figure out whose memory it is."

Then words grew too heavy to say, and even his thoughts felt too heavy to think, and Lee drifted to sleep with one remaining string of words in his ears:

Meet me in the park.

25

GRETCHEN

"HEY. YOU. WHIPPLE."

Gretchen turned too quickly at the sound of her name, and the tread of her shoe caught in mulch, causing her to trip.

"Trouble walking? It's one foot in front of the other." She wished she hadn't turned.

"I think she has trouble talking, too," said Emma.

Dylan laughed unkindly. "Hey, can you even *talk*, Whipple?"

"I talk to people worth talking to," said Gretchen, shrugging up the hood of her coat and concentrating on the school parking lot. She wished Asa would hurry.

Something hard slammed into Gretchen's shoulder. She turned and saw a calculator at her feet. The screen had shattered and the batteries sprung loose.

"Good job," she told Emma and Dylan. "You know those are school property, don't you?"

"So?" said Dylan. "Your dad's rich. He'll buy the school ten more when he hears what you did."

Where was Asa? He had never been so late picking her up from school. Gretchen could keep her mouth shut around Emma and Dylan, but only for so long. She knew exactly what question they both wanted her to ask next.

What did I do? she would ask.

And Dylan would say, *Broke poor Emma's calculator. Who will believe your side of things? You've got the worst detention record in the eighth grade.*

So Gretchen wasn't going to answer them. She'd promised herself: no more demerits. No more acting out. No more paying attention to Emma or Dylan or any of the other orange-table kids. She just wished Emma and Dylan would make it easier on her and leave her alone.

Gretchen shoved her hands deep into her coat pockets, hiding them from the biting wind. Her right knuckles bumped into something rough. She frowned, latched her fingers around the object, and tugged it out.

Of course. How could she have forgotten? It was the piece of coal she had found in Poplar Wood—the coal she had thought at first was a gray fox.

"What's that?" called Emma. "Hey! What's that you got?"

None of your business, Gretchen thought, shoving the coal back into her pocket.

But then the coal wasn't in her pocket. Gretchen's fingers curled in on themselves, clasped around nothing but lining. She frowned and pressed her palm flat. Nothing. It must have fallen out.

Emma screamed.

"Oh my God, Dylan! Do you see that? There, right there!"

Then Dylan screamed.

"Get back inside," he shouted to Emma. "Quick, get back inside!"

Gretchen watched them run into the school, hysterical, but she felt none of their panic. She was strangely calm, and when she turned to face the thing that had scared them, she was not afraid.

Oh yes, she thought. *Of course that's what it is.*

A gray wildcat sat crouched beside her, teeth bared and eyes gleaming. It wasn't baring its teeth at Gretchen, but at the glass doors, where Emma and Dylan stood watching it, blanched with fear.

Gretchen laughed. The whole thing was suddenly funny. She knew that the wildcat wouldn't harm her just as certainly as she knew that the wildcat had very recently been a lump of coal in her pocket. Gretchen had no idea how such a thing was possible, which was why she was laughing. She hadn't imagined that gray fox back in Poplar Wood; it had been the piece of coal all along.

The wildcat stared at Gretchen with yellow eyes. It closed its mouth and made a soft whining sound, as though to apologize for putting on a frightening face before. Then, its ears tensed and flattened. It had heard something, and soon Gretchen heard the sound, too: the sputter of a motorbike engine.

"Asa?"

Gretchen stared at her brother, motionless, even when he pulled his bike to the curb. She saw but didn't hear him shout over the rumbling. Then Asa looked from Gretchen to the wildcat by her side. He cut the engine.

Gretchen turned to her wildcat, but now there was only a lump of coal in the grass.

"What was that?" asked Asa, running to her side.

Gretchen grabbed the coal and shoved it into her pocket.

"What was what?" she asked.

"That thing sitting next to you—where did you find it?"

Gretchen shrugged. "I don't know what you're talking about."

"Get your hand out of your pocket."

Gretchen let go of the coal and showed her empty hand to Asa. But she knew what he would do next, and she wrenched away from him just as he made a grab for her pocket.

"It's not yours!" she shouted. "I found it in the wood, it belongs to me!"

"Stupid," said Asa, but he didn't grab for it again.

"Why were you late?" Gretchen demanded. "Where's Whipplesnapper?"

"Had to take her to the shop. Stop crying, would you?"

"I'm not crying!"

Asa nodded at Gretchen's pocket. "It's not going to stay there forever. Better to let it go now."

"And give it to you?" Gretchen snorted. "Fat chance."

"You don't need to give it to me. It'll find me eventually, because it's *mine*."

Gretchen wondered if any of that was true. Asa could just be trying to steal what was hers for the thrill of it. That was nothing new. Growing up, Asa had stolen plenty of things from Gretchen: twine, red nail polish, a music box that had once belonged to her mother—if something went missing, that just meant Asa had it. The music box was the only thing that Gretchen had gotten back, and only because she'd tattled to Gram.

"I'm going to walk home," said Gretchen, heading for the sidewalk. Asa's footsteps matched her own.

"Not with *that* in your pocket. You can't."

Gretchen sped up, but Asa's hand caught her by the shoulder and turned her around so hard she lost her balance and fell on her backside. Pain burst in her right ankle, and Gretchen cried out. Asa swore.

"God, I'm sorry. I'm sorry, Gretch."

Asa didn't say sorry, not unless Mayor Whipple or Gram forced it out of him. Even then, Asa never *looked* sorry. But that was the way he looked now. He wasn't smiling. His eyes were concerned, and his cheeks were red, and he looked *sorry*. Like he had two weeks ago, when he'd slammed the door in Gretchen's face. Something about that look only made Gretchen angrier.

"I hate you," she said, pressing her hand to the hollow of her ankle.

"Let me help you up." Asa reached out a hand.

"Why did you do that? I hate you. I *hate* you."

"You can't walk on your own."

Gretchen tried. She scooted her feet on the cracked concrete and pushed, hard, with her hands. But the pain shrieked through her ankle again, and stared up at Asa, livid.

"I ha—"

"Hate me. Yeah. Got it. But you still can't walk." He stooped by her side. "If I carry you, promise not to bite?"

"No," Gretchen muttered, but she let Asa wrap one arm around her back and hoist her into his grip.

He carried her with no difficulty. Gretchen found that Asa's chest was very wide and his arms strong.

"I'm setting you down now," said a voice with no face, now that Gretchen's eyes were closed. The dark world around her felt unreal, and time seemed to be moving very fast and very slow at once.

Something hard and uncomfortable came down on her head. A helmet. Fingers latched a buckle under Gretchen's chin, and the strap pinched, but she said nothing. Her ankle was still hurting worse than that.

It could be broken, Gretchen thought, and found she must've said so, because Asa answered, "It isn't. At worst, it's sprained."

Then Gretchen found herself wrapping arms around something solid and leather, and wind was blowing in her face. And then there was warmth and water on her foot. Then something unbearably cold was in her grip, and a voice she did not like was telling her to hold it against her ankle. And slowly, the pain subsided.

And Gretchen opened her eyes.

And everything came into focus.

They were at home, in the parlor. Asa was sitting on the couch, next to her. A sandwich bag filled with ice cubes lay atop Gretchen's ankle, which was propped on a pillow on the couch. Gretchen eyed a scar running across Asa's right palm—the same hand that had been bandaged at Essie's burial. He noticed her looking and closed his hand up.

"So you found it in the wood?" Asa shook his head. "I lost it there. I guess I shouldn't be surprised it found you."

Gretchen realized she was no longer wearing her coat. "Where's my coal?" she demanded.

"Just there."

Gretchen looked, and by the fireplace, a small gray cat sat washing its face. It looked at Gretchen with alert yellow eyes, then returned to licking its paw.

"It's not *coal*," said Asa, "and it's not yours. I'm the one who bought it."

"I don't believe you," said Gretchen. "Why should I?"

Asa smiled all wrongly. "Because I bought it from Death."

Gretchen stared, uncomprehending. "You mean . . . you did a Rite? But . . . how? "

"For one thing, I'm the firstborn." Asa raised an eyebrow pointedly.

Gretchen had nothing to say to this.

Asa motioned to the cat, which had curled itself into a tight, purring ball atop the atlas on the coffee table. "What do you see there?"

"A cat."

"But it wasn't always a cat."

"No. When I saw it in Poplar Wood, it was a fox. In the parking lot, it was a . . . mountain lion, I think. And in between, it's that piece of coal."

"Stone," corrected Asa. "It's a Wishing Stone. Did you know every town's set of Shades has one to sell? All it takes is a Rite."

Gretchen looked at the cat again, only now it was not a cat but a stone, smooth and black, resting atop a detailed map of Cairo.

"I don't get it," she said. "What does it do?"

"In theory, it grants wishes. But it works different than I thought it would. It's not like a magic lantern. You don't say your wish out loud. Whatever you're feeling deepest inside, that's what the stone takes to be your wish. That's what it grants. And in the meantime, it does what it wants, takes whatever shape it pleases."

Gretchen looked again to the stone, only this time it had vanished completely, and she jumped so suddenly she sent a rush of pain through her foot. Wincing, she readjusted the bag of ice. "Where did it go?"

"Wherever it wants to be." Asa was glaring into the fireplace. "Whatever you think that stone is, it's not."

Gretchen considered this. "Asa. Why did you do that Rite? What did you need to wish for?"

Asa kept his dark eyes on the fire. "It doesn't matter anymore."

"What was Death like, in person? The Rite lets you see him, doesn't it?"

Asa rose from his seat. "I said, it doesn't matter."

His words were cold, the way Gretchen was used to, and she found she was almost relieved by the change. This version of Asa she knew, and there was a strange comfort in his meanness.

Asa walked to the parlor door. When he reached it, he said, "Leave it alone, Gretch, and don't touch it again. I mean it. I told you, it thinks for itself."

Gretchen watched Asa leave the room. Then, looking back to her ankle, she saw it: a small gray hare was sitting at her feet, rapidly sniffing at the couch's velvet upholstery. She reached out, as though to catch it, but the moment her hand touched its fur, the hare transformed once more, turning small and stony in her palm.

She'd heard Asa's warning, and she meant to heed it.

Only not quite yet.

26
—
FELIX

"When did you first see blood?"

"Day ago. Got here quick as I could. Melvin told me if anyone could cure it up, it'd be you, sir."

Felix stood in the corner of the examination room, watching as Vince made small talk with his patient, a miner from Cullman Gully.

"Please," he told the man, "call me Vince."

The miner regarded his doctor with caution. He hadn't taken his eyes off Vince since he had arrived at the back door. His face was bearded and grizzled, but his eyes shone a clear green that reminded Felix of mint. He smelled of gasoline, and his hair was slicked back from a sweaty brow. The man was, in fact, drenched in sweat. It trickled along his temples and beaded on his knuckles and dampened his shirt in muscle-guided patterns.

The miner noticed Felix looking at him, and his mint eyes lightened. He smiled kindly as though to say *Don't worry too much about little old me.*

Felix didn't want this man to die.

"When did the fever begin?" Vince asked his patient.

"Four days back, I reckon, I started feeling poorly. Would've come earlier, but my wife Betsy, she don't much like the idea of my seeing you. No offense, but some folk say you've made a pact with the devil."

Vince looked up, not at the miner, but at Death, who was standing on the threshold, peeling white evening gloves from his hands. What did Death dress so well for, Felix wondered, when death was the most ordinary of events?

Vince tucked in the earpieces of his stethoscope and with a grim smile said, "I might very well have done."

"Well, ain't my place to judge, 'specially if you give me the cure all them others talk about."

From a pocket inside his fine jacket, Death pulled out metal pincers. The miner heaved out a cough so violent his shoulders jerked forward, and a spray of crimson showered on his collar.

"Felix," said Vince, "why don't you offer the good man something to drink?"

He's going to die, thought Felix. *There's nothing to be done about it now.*

Felix's job in the examination room was to comfort the patients, to keep them at ease.

"We can't change a thing once Death is at work," his father always told him. "All we can do is make the passing more bearable."

So Felix now handed a mug of hot spearmint tea to the miner, to do just that.

"Kind of you," said the man, once the coughs had subsided, "but whiskey would've been more welcome, eh?"

The miner turned to Vince with a smile, but his doctor no longer smiled back. Death had moved to the foot of the table.

27
LEE

Lee had told no one about the memories hidden beneath his bed. He couldn't possibly admit to his mother what he had done. Felix and Lee still hadn't spoken since Felix's punishment. As for Gretchen, Lee wanted to be cautious. It was possible those remaining two jars contained nothing at all to do with Essie Hasting, and it was better not to get Gretchen's hopes up. Anyway, if Lee told Gretchen, she'd butt in and pepper him with a million questions, and Lee didn't want to deal with that.

After breaking the first jar, Lee had felt off-kilter—often nauseated and always faint, as though his joints were not quite connected the way they ought to have been. But on Wednesday morning—the day Gretchen was referring to as "the Book of Rites Heist"—he woke with a clear mind and sturdy stomach. When he returned home from school, he locked himself in his bedroom, determined to open another memory jar.

No patients had visited his mother that day, so Lee didn't have any obligations between now and eight o'clock, when he'd promised to meet Gretchen. He knew this memory might make him sick again, but Lee hoped the worst of that was over. Maybe, he reasoned, absorbing someone else's memories was a little like running: If you kept doing it, you built up endurance.

Lee sat on the edge of his bed, clasping the second of the jars. His mother often warned him that memories were fragile, capricious things. When she extracted them from her patients, the work had to be done under Memory's supervision. The process was calculated and invariable: Judith placed both hands on the patient's forehead, eyes closed in concentration. Slowly, she siphoned out the memory from the patient's mind. It emerged from the ear and flowed through midair, a ribbon of shimmering liquid. Then, in its suspended form, the memory circled and funneled itself into the waiting jar. When the process was complete, Judith quickly sealed shut the lid, lest the memory escape to her own mind or to oblivion.

Though Lee had misshelved memories and written sloppy labels, very few memories had escaped under his watch. Now, he was letting loose memories *on purpose*.

"But it isn't wrong," Lee whispered. "Not if it's for a good cause. And if Gretchen holds up her end of the deal, I have to hold up mine. That's how a deal works. Quid pro quo."

This time, he would pay close attention, make note of everything he saw while the memory was at its freshest. And this time, one way or another, he'd find out whose memories these were. It had to be a student at Boone Ridge High—that Lee knew. But not a friend, or at least, no one Essie readily spoke to in public.

Lee studied the memory in his hands. He'd broken the first jar when its contents were still bubbling, and they had evaporated into his consciousness. He wondered if this next memory would behave the same way, now that it was cooled and gelatinous. Would he have to dash it to the ground like the first jar? Would he merely have to unscrew the lid and breathe deeply? Or would he have to—Lee shuddered at this thought—*drink* the thick, black liquid?

"You're not going to figure it out by staring," he told himself. "You've just got to open it and see."

Lee's hands shook as he turned the lid. Steel screeched against glass like a warning.

"I don't care," said Lee. "I don't."

He unscrewed the lid entirely and set it aside. Then he peered inside the jar. The smell was unexpected. It was not at all foul, but earthy, a mixture of leaves and turned soil and still water. And Lee was no longer inhaling the scent in his bedroom but in the shade of hickory trees. Across from him, sitting on the damp grass, was Essie Hasting.

"I knew I could tell you," she said, her voice soft and wet. She was crying, he realized. A fat tear fell to her sneaker and soaked its neon lace. "I know what your family thinks of people like me. But I couldn't help it. I didn't have a choice."

"I know," he said.

He wanted to wrap his arms around Essie, offer her something solid and warm to hold on to. But he wasn't in the practice of touching anybody, and he didn't know where to begin. He reached out, then panicked, and dropped his hand, where it landed awkwardly on Essie's ankle. A new tear fell and splashed onto his skin. And suddenly he didn't feel awkward anymore. He felt needed. He felt right. His fingers curled around the delicate bone of Essie's ankle.

"It's not so terrible most of the time," she said. "I just do what Passion asks. It's never anything bad—only a bunch of silly matchmaking tasks, delivering flowers where I'm told."

"And what? They work like Cupid's arrows?"

"Don't look at me that way."

"I'm not," he said, squeezing her ankle again. "I'm trying to understand."

Essie nodded limply. "Like Cupid's arrows, sure, more or less. If you think of it that way, I guess that makes me . . . Cupid's bow."

"Flowers," he said. "So what, red roses or something?"

Essie opened her backpack and reached inside, motioning for him to give her his hand. In it, Essie placed a bright purple flower.

"If you hold it close and concentrate," she said, "you'll know who your love is."

He snorted. "What if I don't believe in true love?"

"It doesn't matter what you believe. Anyway, I didn't say true love. It just shows you who your love is at the moment."

"So more like your crush."

He ran his thumb along the flower's petals, then offered it back to Essie, but she shook her head.

"You can keep it."

"Okay," he said. "Thanks."

He wondered if she knew. Could she tell, just by looking at someone, who they loved?

Could she tell how much he loved her?

"I didn't mean to cry on you." Essie patted at her eyes. "That isn't what we came for."

"We don't have to do this today, if you don't want."

"Are you kidding? I've been looking forward to this all week. Whenever I try to bring up things like this with my mother, she won't listen. She thinks there's only one way to do things. The Hasting way."

"And you?"

Essie looked hesitant. "When I was in Chattanooga, I looked up the summoners who lived there."

"Essie, you didn't—"

"And they don't keep their Rites locked in glass boxes. They're willing to share them, all you have to do is pay. So I told them what I could afford, and what I wanted to do, and they gave me these."

Essie removed something from her backpack. It was a notebook, small and thin.

"We can do it, Asa," she said, excitedly. "All we have to do is wish for it."

A sound, distant and staccato, crackled in his ear.

He shook his head, trying to clear it away, but it only grew louder and louder and—

Lee returned to his bedroom with a choking start, gripping the quilt on his bed.

Asa.

Essie had called him *Asa.* These were Asa Whipple's violet-ribboned memories.

Had *Asa* been friends with Essie Hasting? Had he even . . . *loved* her? It hardly seemed possible. Essie was a popular, cheery girl. And Asa was . . . *Asa.* A snarling, motorbike-riding, bad kid. He was a summoner, and Essie had been an apprentice. Although, Lee reflected, was that an impossibility? Wasn't he himself hanging out with Gretchen Whipple?

Gretchen.

He had to tell her about the memories now.

"Leander!"

His mother's voice was outside his bedroom door. Lee wiped at his eyes and stumbled to his feet.

"Coming—er, hold on!"

The memory jar, now drained of its contents, was still in his hand. Hurriedly, he shoved it beneath the bed.

"Everything all right?"

Lee crossed the room and opened the door, still blinking back fog from his eyes. Judith stood wiping flour-covered hands on her skirt. She looked worried, and Lee realized he must have appeared as out of sorts as he felt.

"Sorry," he said. "I was reading. Must've fallen asleep."

Judith's face was still creased with concern. "The two of you are fighting, aren't you?" she asked.

"W-what? What makes you think that?"

"Come out here. Memory is out for a walk, and I'd like to speak with you in private."

This was how Lee found himself wrapped in a knit shawl on the parlor couch, where most of Judith's patients sat. He sipped cocoa from a pewter mug that warmed his hands almost to the point of pain. Though Lee was dizzy, the cocoa's heat helped ground him. Judith sat across from Lee, like he was one of her patients.

"I know something is the matter," she said. "You haven't gone out to the conservatory for days straight."

Lee stared at his cocoa and did not reply.

"Is this about that Whipple girl?"

"What?" Lee looked up sharply. "No, of course not!"

Lee felt bad for lying to his mother, but she simply couldn't know he was hanging out with a Whipple *on purpose*, let alone making a deal with one.

"Leander," she said. "You can tell me—"

"I'm *fine*," Lee interrupted, cross at the use of his full name. "It's Felix who isn't okay."

Judith set down her mug and leaned in close. "What's wrong with him?"

"He got into trouble."

"With Death?"

Lee nodded. "I didn't want to tell you, because I knew you'd worry. I've seen him around since, but he won't talk to me about it. So I've left him alone."

Judith's eyes were sad, and Lee could not look at them without feeling sad himself.

"A troubled young man came to this house recently," she said. "No one so young should possess a memory as terrible as his. It was full of loss and guilt. He's better off with it extracted, of course, but even with the extraction, there will always be a residue within him. He'll never be able to fully shake the feelings the memory created. And the worst of it is, the events of that memory were entirely his own doing."

Lee latched his fingers together, concentrated on staring at his thumbs.

"Lee," said his mother, "you will make mistakes. Unwittingly, you will make terrible decisions, and no matter how hard you try to protect yourself, you will fall into bad times. But I dearly hope no son of mine will ever *choose* to go down a path that creates a foul memory. That you would choose to not speak to your brother."

"But you don't understand! If you *knew* Felix, you'd know how difficult he can be, when he doesn't talk, when he won't—" Lee stopped short, for he'd said precisely the wrong words. His mother would never know Felix. She'd never have the chance.

Judith took Lee's hands and held them in her own.

"You love your brother," she said, "and there is nothing so awful in this wide world as to be separated from someone you love. Now, why would you do that to yourself willingly?"

"Mom," Lee said. "Do you ever stop missing him?"

"No. I will miss them both as long as I live."

"But how can you miss Felix when you don't know him?"

"I carried you both inside me, him just as much as you. And do not tell me you don't miss your father just because you've never known *him*."

Lee grew quiet at the thought. Of course his mother was right: He missed his father with an inextinguishable love, even though he'd never seen his face.

Lee knew she was right about him and Felix, too.

"Still," he said. "The silence is all Felix's doing."

"That may be," his mother said, "but it doesn't mean making it right can't be *your* doing."

Then she rose and took away his mug, even though it was still half-full.

The clock on the mantle chimed the quarter hour. Lee had set out for the Whipple house before it chimed again.

28
GRETCHEN

BECAUSE I BOUGHT *it from Death.*

Asa's voice still rang in Gretchen's ears. Her brother had done a Rite. *Asa* had done a Rite with *Death.* Even now, she attempted to process these facts, but sheer excitement made it near impossible. She sat on the back terrace of Whipple House, bundled in a puffy coat and nestled into a lawn chair. According to her watch, it was 7:56. Four minutes till Lee was due.

Gretchen knew it was a risk, inviting a Vickery to her house when the family was at home, but there was simply no other way. Her father kept his keys in his office, and he kept his office locked whenever he was away. So Gretchen couldn't steal the key to the Book of Rites unless Mayor Whipple was home, and Mayor

Whipple was only at home early in the morning and at night. Nighttime had seemed the better option. It would be risky, yes, but she had a plan. And now, holding a small stone in her cupped hands, Gretchen had a new plan. A *better* plan.

Before, she was going to be the one to distract her father, calling him out into the hall while Lee snuck into the office and snatched the key ring. Gretchen had been nervous about this approach, because Lee had never been in the office nor seen the keys, as Gretchen had. It would take him longer, and there was the chance he'd be caught, and she didn't want to imagine what her father would do if he found a Vickery snooping in his private office.

But now, Gretchen thought in triumph, the Wishing Stone could provide the distraction while *she* stole the keys and Lee served as lookout. It was a faster plan, and safer too. Maybe Asa would be angry if he knew what she was up to, but Gretchen really did mean to get rid of the Wishing Stone when it was all over.

She checked her watch again: 7:59. Gretchen strained her eyes in the dim terrace light, looking for movement. And there *was* movement, she found, though not the kind she'd been expecting. Little bits of movement that caught in the light—objects small and quick and everywhere at once.

Snow.

It was early in the season for it. Normally, Boone Ridge didn't see so much as a flake until deep into January. Gretchen grinned. She was going to take this snow to be a good omen, a sign that her plan would work.

"Gretchen!"

On instinct, she closed one hand over the Wishing Stone, holding it tight. Then she waved at the boy running up—not as a welcome, but as a frantic sign to keep his voice down.

"Shhh!" she said, as Lee came to a stop before her, slapping his hands on his knees. She wondered if he'd run here all the way from Poplar Wood.

"My family's all here," she whispered. "We've got to be quiet."

Lee nodded, apologetic, gulping down breath. Gretchen was eager to tell her news about Asa and the Wishing Stone, but Lee looked like words were straining to burst from him like steam from a boiling kettle.

"Well?" Gretchen pressed.

Lee shook his head, and at last, he pushed out breathless speech, his eyes aglow.

"Asa. Your brother. He and Essie Hasting . . . they were *friends*."

29
FELIX

DEATH HAD SENT Felix to gather herbs many times before, but never this late, and never on so cold a night as this.

One glance at Death was all it took for Felix to know he was not forgiven yet, not even after two nights in the cellar. Death never looked angry, exactly. Not in the way one would expect a human face to look angry. At all times, his lips remained thin and pale, his shoulders straight. Those features never altered. What changed were the eyes. Felix had tried to explain it once to Lee, with little success.

"It's not a change of color," he had said, "or the size of his pupils. It's something else. Something changes there that does not change in real people, like you and me. I know it's a *something else*, but there isn't a word for it."

The explanation was as far beyond Felix as if Lee had asked him to explain what the color green *felt* like. But even though he could not explain them, he knew the meanings of those eye shifts. And so he'd seen Death's eyes and known: Death had not forgiven him.

Vince knew it, too. He stood on the back porch as Felix readied to leave for the wood in search of the red chrysanthemums Death had demanded.

"I cannot stop him," he said to his son. "Felix, you understand, don't you? I don't want you to go out there, but Death is my master as much as he is yours."

Felix said nothing.

His father caught him by the elbow and knelt so that their eyes met. He placed something warm in Felix's hand. It was bacon, wrapped in wax paper. Felix stashed the food in his satchel but made no show of gratitude; he only switched on his electric lantern.

"Be careful," Vince said, and Felix looked at his father then, anger boiling in his heart.

"I wish you'd never met Mom," he said. "I wish she'd never had me. I didn't choose to be an apprentice, and you shouldn't have either. You should've been okay to stay unhappy all on your own, without bringing me into it."

Vince's face twisted up, and Felix couldn't stand to look at it. He ran down the steps, into the dark wood.

It had been wrong to say those things. Felix knew that even as they were passing from his lips. He was angry, *so angry*, but not with his father. Not really. It had been Death who had hurt them both and Death who was hurting them still.

Felix walked into the night, and the snow started up shortly after. He searched an hour straight for the red chrysanthemums. It was a new moon tonight, so the wilds of the wood were black as they could be, and it was slow going with nothing but his lantern for light.

As Felix trudged on, the snow picked up. The wind was strong, and flakes kept whipping into his face and melting down his cheeks. At last, two hours into the search, Felix settled his sore, cold limbs beneath a bare oak tree.

"I'm not yours yet," he said. "You can't have me, Death. You can't just *claim* people for yourself, like we belong to you, like property. You can't just trick us into giving our lives away, and you're not going to anymore. If the Agreement can be broken, then I'm going to break it."

They were terrible words, but powerful ones. Here, in the wood, as Felix shivered and ached over an errand that was a punishment, he was not afraid to say them out loud.

If the Agreement could be broken, if a Whipple could be trusted, if the Rites were real . . .

If.

If, then everything might change.

30
LEE

GRETCHEN GAPED AT Lee. "What—what did you say?"

"Essie." Lee panted. "And Asa. They were friends. And I think . . . um, I think that . . . maybe they were . . . in love."

Gretchen blinked. "You're crazy. Essie and *Asa*?"

Powdery bits of snow fell around them, catching on the fringes of Gretchen's black hair. Lee's lungs were burning from running so fast and for so long; his stomach was lurching, and his vision was splotched. He reflected that maybe he shouldn't have run so soon after absorbing another memory.

"I know it sounds crazy," Lee admitted, "but I saw it for myself."

"How?"

"I . . . I may have . . . looked at Asa's memories."

"Sorry, what?"

Lee had not considered how difficult this would be—telling Gretchen about the memories he'd stolen when they belonged to her *brother*. Still, he tried his best, explaining to her about the broken jar and the memories he had seen and the one remaining jar he had yet to open.

"And they were planning something," he finished. "That notebook you found in Hickory Park was Essie's. She's the one who wrote down all those Rites."

"But," said Gretchen, who looked very pale, "where did she get them?"

"She said she bought them from other summoners. She and Asa were using the Rites to ask for something, I'm not sure what. But whatever it was, I think maybe Death killed Essie for it."

Gretchen's face paled further. "The Wishing Stone," she whispered.

"What?"

"Asa told me he did a Rite with Death. He bought a Wishing Stone."

"What's that?"

"Something that gives you what you wish for. But what were they wishing for, that's the question. . . . "

Gretchen met Lee's gaze. "Vickery, I think we're on to something here. But we're on a tight schedule. My dad is in his office, so we've got to act now. And then I've got some news for *you*."

Lee wasn't sure he would ever breathe right again.

He was inside the office of Mayor Whipple—*the* Mayor Whipple—peering out in case the man himself should round the corner. His heart was hammering, filling his ears with a quick *thump-thump-thump*. He hadn't been able to catch his breath from the time he'd begun running to the time he told Gretchen about Essie Hasting to the time Gretchen opened her hand and explained to him what a Wishing Stone was.

"It'll help us," she'd said. "It gives you what you wish deep down, and what I wish deep down is to figure out what happened to Essie. And the first step to doing *that* is to get my dad out of his office."

Lee had stared at the stone with far less confidence. "But it's a rock."

"No, it's the *Wishing Stone*."

"But how did you—"

Gretchen had raised a hand. "You're not the only one uncovering juicy secrets, Vickery."

That had been the end of that. Gretchen had told Lee he would be the lookout, ensuring that no one came into the office. Then she'd stepped inside the house and set the coal-like stone on the floor, straightened, and closed her eyes. If Lee hadn't known better, he would have thought Gretchen was praying.

Then, in one blink, the stone vanished from the floor, and in its place stood a very large dog. It was a light gray Saint Bernard with darker gray spots. Suddenly, the dog took off, lumbering down the hallway. Through the glass doors, Lee heard Gretchen shout, "Dad, quick! There's a dog in the house!"

Gretchen ran out of sight, and as she did, Lee noticed a limp in her gait. Only a few seconds later she was back at the door and waving Lee inside.

"Quick," she said. "This is it."

They ran for her father's office.

Now, as Lee stood at the doorway, he could hear the sounds of a commotion from another part of the house—a man shouting, and an older women crying out, and the sounds of objects toppling and glass shattering.

"Confound it! What in the Sam Hill is this!" shouted Mayor Whipple.

Even though it was hard enough to breathe, and Lee thought his heart might break from fright, he found himself giggling. The whole thing suddenly struck him as ridiculous. Here he was, helping a Whipple steal from another Whipple, all with the help of a magical Saint Bernard! Lee managed to swallow his laughter as Gretchen opened and shut desk drawers with lightning speed.

"Any luck?" he whispered.

That's when he heard the clinking of metal. Gretchen's determined face turned radiant, and she held up the key ring.

But Lee couldn't breathe just yet. They were only half done.

He scanned the hallway once more. The commotion now seemed to be coming from right above their heads.

"Coast is clear," he said.

They ran from the office, down the hallway and into the library.

"Okay," said Gretchen, approaching the locked-up Book of Rites. "Okay, okay."

She grabbed the lock of the glass box and attempted to fit the first of the keys inside. It slid into place but did not turn. Gretchen grunted, wiggled it out, and tried the next. There were at least a dozen keys on the ring. From down the hall, Lee heard the Saint Bernard bark.

The second key did not work, nor the third. Gretchen swore as she tried the fourth. It fit. And then, it clicked.

Lee jumped. "You got it?"

Gretchen slid the lock from its place. She opened the door of the glass box, and as she did, her grin stretched as far as a grin could go.

"That's it," she said, reaching in and—with more tenderness than Lee had expected from Gretchen—removing the Book of Rites.

There was a *crash* from down the hall, and a series of playful barks.

"Come back here, you mongrel!"

The Wishing-Stone-turned-Saint-Bernard had led Mayor Whipple back downstairs.

Gretchen's grin vanished. She dropped the book in Lee's hands.

"Go," she said. "Outside. Wait for me there."

"But if your dad—"

"*Go!*" Gretchen shoved Lee toward the library door. He glanced back once, to see that Gretchen had yanked another large book from one of the shelves and set it inside the glass case. Any close look would show that the stand-in was most certainly not the Book of Rites, but it would satisfy a passing glance for a couple days. And all they needed was a couple days.

Lee hurried down the hall, squeezing the book to his chest. When he reached the terrace, at last, Lee breathed in all the way, and, hidden in an alcove, he felt his heart stop pounding quite so loud. He held the book before him. It was old and tattered, made of browned pages, and sat heavy in Lee's hands. The cover read, in faded gold leaf, *Book of Rites*.

If Lee's apprenticing ancestors could see him now.

Minutes passed. Lee was too nervous to sit and too petrified to pace. He stood in the dark of the stone alcove, waiting, hoping Gretchen had not been caught. And if she had been, then what? Would she tell Mayor Whipple everything? Would she rat Lee out? Had that been her plan all along?

The French doors swung open, and Lee froze. What were Vickeries and Whipples supposed to do if they found the other stealing private property? Would Mayor Whipple torture Lee? Lock him up? Lee thought again of the Hatfields and McCoys.

"Lee?"

It was Gretchen. She peered around the alcove where he hid, an almost-smile on her face.

"What're you doing *there*?" she asked, but didn't wait for an answer. "I got the keys back to his desk, and just then . . . guess what? Dad hollered that the dog had *disappeared*."

"Do Wishing Stones do that?" asked Lee. "Just disappear?"

"I don't know," Gretchen admitted. "All I know is it's nowhere to be found now—dog or stone. And the house is a wreck. Gram is beside herself, keeps saying it's the work of anarchists. I guess it's true that Wishing Stones aren't what you expect them to be."

Lee got a feeling that Gretchen was now speaking to herself and not to him. He held the book out to her.

"We did it." Gretchen looked at Lee, the almost-smile growing. "You did good, Vickery."

Lee couldn't help himself. He smiled, all the way. "Yeah, you too . . . Whipple."

For some reason, he couldn't breathe again.

"We've got a lot to talk about," Gretchen whispered, "but I have got to get back in there. Gram is blowing a gasket, and it'll look fishy if I'm gone."

She shoved the book back into Lee's chest.

"What—what're you doing?" he asked.

"You keep it safe. No way I can sneak it upstairs now."

"But—but—"

Lee knew there was a good reason for him not to take the Book of Rites, but at the moment that reason wasn't coming to him.

"I trust you, Vickery." Gretchen looked him in the eye. "I *can* trust you, right?"

Lee swallowed, speechless. He nodded.

"Then okay. Keep the book safe, and tomorrow night, eight o'clock sharp, meet me at the bleachers. We'll make a plan. One that takes into account all this new information." She pointed a finger in his face. "And don't you dare double-cross me."

Lee watched as Gretchen hurried away, still with that limp in her step, and it was only after she had slipped into the house that the protests filled his mind:

You can't expect me, a Vickery, to take the Book of Rites home.

I don't want to walk through the dark wood again.

Make what plan?

But it was too late to do anything but walk away with the Book of Rites clutched in his arms.

31
FELIX

FELIX HAD STILL not found the chrysanthemums. It was long past midnight, and he had spent hours in the cold, circling Poplar Wood and casting his lantern light into every nook and burrow, peeling away tangled vines and thorny shrubs without success. The snow had picked up and begun to stick on the night-cooled ground, and Felix had been forced to head back to the house. He did not want to return home empty-handed, but he knew that he would be of even less use if he got lost in this wood and froze to death.

Felix found the cellar door was shut and latched, a sure sign Death was below, retired for the evening. He crept to his bedroom and set his alarm clock for dawn, when he would find the flowers with the aid of the sun. And maybe by morning, the snow would have stopped.

"Felix?"

Felix peered out from his bedroom doorway. Vince stood down the hall, in the kitchen. He looked large there, a hulking outline with no features.

"I'm going out tomorrow," Felix said. "I swear, I am. I'll find them. It just got so dark and cold, and the snow was falling so fast I didn't think I'd be able to—"

His father strode toward him, but Felix shrank back.

"Felix," Vince whispered. "Are you afraid of me, too?"

Felix wiped at his raw, running nose. "I thought you'd be mad at me."

His father's arms were suddenly around him, and Felix's breath caught. Then he closed his eyes and rested his head against a familiar knit sweater. Beneath the warmth, he could hear the faint *thrum-thrum* of his father's heart.

"I can't stand to see you suffer," Vince said. "You were right, Felix. This was meant to be my burden. Mine and no one else's."

"Then why did you even have me?"

Felix discovered that he was crying, and crying hard. The effort pushed out too much breath—gasp after gasp. His father lifted him clean off the ground, into his bedroom, and onto his bed.

"I'm sorry, Felix," he said, sitting beside him. "I'm sorry you were born into this life. I thought that with you at least, Death might be kinder."

"But he's not kind at all," said Felix. "And I'd rather die than be his apprentice, like you. You're not happy, are you? You hate what he makes you do, I know you do. So what kind of life is that?"

"It isn't a life I chose willingly, Felix. I wasn't even meant to be Death's apprentice. I wasn't the firstborn; my brother Jeremiah was. But he passed away when we were young."

Felix's father had never told him this, and Felix suddenly experienced the sort of sick he felt when he had gone too long without eating.

"How old were you?" he asked.

"I was six."

"How did he—?" Felix swallowed his first question and tried another one. "Were you scared?"

"Very. And as I grew older, that fear turned to anger. I was angry with my father for signing his own contract. I was angry with my cousins and friends for escaping my fate. I was even angry with my brother for dying. I was a very angry young man. I was until I met a certain girl."

The sick feeling grew stronger. "Mom?"

Vince nodded.

"You never meant for Lee and me to come along, did you?"

"I thought that I would be the one to suffer most from the Agreement. I didn't think through what it would do to you, Felix. Your life has been harder than your brother's, and it's bound to get harder still."

Felix said nothing. He had always known that his life was the harder one, but hearing that said out loud, spoken by someone else—somehow, that made him feel better. Not a great deal, but it was something.

"I realized tonight," said Vince, "I may not be Death, but living under him means that his actions become, in some part, my own. When I stand idly by at his punishments, it's as good as if I myself threw you into the cellar or sent you out in the dead of night."

"But you can't do anything," said Felix. "You're his apprentice, you have to obey him."

"I'm a bad man, Felix."

Felix looked up at his father. "I don't think that. What I said earlier . . . I was angry."

"No. You were right. The Agreement was painful for me, but it was good, too. It kept what I loved alive. It gave me you. But for you . . . for you it's only painful."

Felix did not know how to reply. "I'm tired," he said, honestly.

"Then good night, my boy." His father kissed him on the forehead and left the room.

Felix wondered if he should feel sad, or confused, or angry. He thought that perhaps he ought to feel all of those things. But at the moment, the only feeling left in him was exhaustion.

He fell asleep fully clothed, down to his boots.

32
GRETCHEN

"CHIFFON, JOLENE! I said chiff-*on*!"

It was Thanksgiving Day, and Gram Whipple stood at the foyer balcony, a fearsome thing to behold. Her cotton-white hair was rolled up in curlers, her silk dressing gown sashed in a double-knotted bow. She leaned over the bannister as she yelled, her face contorted into an expression that Gretchen knew very well indeed. Gretchen also knew very well what to do when she encountered that particular expression: stay out of Gram's way.

Jolene, the new event coordinator from the mayor's office, was enduring the full force of Gram, who was on a rampage after discovering that Jolene had ordered tulle and not chiffon for the bannister hangings. Gretchen felt bad for Jolene, but not *too* bad, because she got to go home at five o'clock, whereas Gretchen would be subjected to at least an hour of Gram's griping over supper that night. She was already in a particularly foul mood after the havoc the mysterious Saint Bernard had wreaked on the house the night before. The dog had shattered two vases, turned over an antique armoire, and even knocked family portraits from the walls— most notably Gram's own portrait, painted when she was a young socialite decked in diamonds.

"It's a sabotage!" Gram had cried the night before, pacing the parlor as Mayor Whipple spoke to Sheriff Moser on the phone. "Some ruffian broke into our house and let that horrible creature loose!"

No one had an explanation for how Mayor Whipple had trapped the dog in the pantry, only to open the door and find it gone. Vanished.

No one save Gretchen, of course—and Asa. She'd felt his eyes on her as they sat in the parlor, forced to endure Gram's tirade. Asa knew what the Saint Bernard was and why it had disappeared, and he knew Gretchen had used it on purpose, though he didn't know why. She didn't meet his gaze the entire night. She said nothing when Gram finally released them to their bedrooms, and Asa said nothing to her.

Gretchen felt guilty, which was an odd sensation. She rarely felt guilty, whether she was in trouble with Gram or with the school counselor. She'd certainly never felt guilty when it came to Asa. He was the bad one. The cruel one. The guilty one.

Only now, Gretchen wasn't sure what to think. In recent days, she had seen flashes of an Asa she did not recognize—a kind, almost *caring* brother. And now her mind was abuzz with what Lee had told her yesterday: Asa had known Essie Hasting. They had been working on something together. Maybe he had even been in Hickory Park when Essie had died.

Gretchen didn't know what to make of these facts, no matter how she snipped and stitched them together. She only knew that Asa had shared something important with Gretchen. He had told her a secret and acted kind—as kind as Asa could be, anyway. In return, Gretchen had ignored his warning. The guilt had been stinging inside her chest ever since. But then, her ankle had been stinging, too. And Asa was the reason for her hurt foot, Gretchen reminded herself, as though this fact justified her use of the Wishing Stone.

Thanksgiving was just another reason why Gretchen wished she weren't the daughter of an important man. Movies and television shows made Thanksgiving seem like such a pleasant time for other families. It was supposed to be one long day of feasting and card games and football and running around piles of leaves in golden afternoon light. But Thanksgiving hadn't ever been that in the Whipple household. No relatives came into town; Gram was the only surviving grandparent, and Gretchen had neither aunts nor uncles to speak of, and therefore no cousins. The Whipples didn't play card games or run around. Thanksgiving only meant that Gretchen had a few days off school and that, instead of a big meal, the Whipples were left to scavenge the kitchen for food while Gram began her party preparations. Because the *real* event at Whipple House wasn't Thanksgiving Day but the Christmas gala that took place just two days later.

As Gram annually reminded the family, the gala was *everything*. Everyone who was anyone attended the party, from several Tennessee state senators to the governor of West Virginia to Jessup White, a local millionaire. It was an extraordinary turnout for so small a town as Boone Ridge. Each year's gala had to be perfect and, moreover, better than the last one.

Mayor Whipple had the easiest job of it. In the days leading up to the gala, he stayed at his downtown office, often straight through suppertime. He claimed the overtime was work-related, but Gretchen had seen him stumble tipsily up the driveway more than once on a late November night, calling out to the suited, laughing men who dropped him off. She was jealous that her father was the only one who could really dodge Gram's sour mood, but then she also thought it was sad that a grown man could still be afraid of his own mother.

All that morning, Gretchen had done as Gram had asked her, polishing silver and scrubbing floors and dusting furniture in the places the family didn't even use, like the back parlor and the guest bedrooms. Gretchen knew when she'd put in enough work for Gram to not throw a fit. If she followed orders for the morning and early afternoon, Gram would leave her alone for the rest of Thanksgiving. That was why Gretchen had chosen tonight to meet with Lee. That was why she was escaping now.

Asa was at the top of the stairs, lying with his head hanging off the top step. He was listening to music, a slamming bass raging out of his headphones. Asa's only responsibility that day had been to rake up the leaves in the yard, a task he'd accomplished within an hour. Now he seemed so positively deadened to the world, Gretchen wondered if she might sneak past without him noticing. She tiptoed up the stairs, and when she reached her brother, she stretched her foot over his shoulder, touching the carpet with just the tip of her sneaker.

Asa's eyes snapped open.

Gretchen shrieked, stumbling down the top two stairs. Her hurt ankle throbbed in protest, and Gretchen cursed. Asa sat up, his hair staticky from the carpet, a mess of black curls. He yanked off his headphones, fixing an even glare on Gretchen.

"What's wrong with you?" he asked.

"You're in my way."

Asa smiled. "So?"

What would Asa say if he knew Gretchen had stolen the Book of Rites? Would he be proud of her? Or would he yell at her and yank her arm the way he had in Hickory Park? She could still feel the hard grip of his fingers and his cold, sharp words: *There won't be a next time.*

What would Asa say if Gretchen asked him, right here, about Essie Hasting? Would he deny it, grow angry, yell? Would he explain why he'd lied about knowing her? But no, Gretchen stopped and reflected. Asa had never said that he hadn't known Essie. Gretchen had simply never asked; that possibility hadn't seemed remotely possible. As to the other thing Lee had said, about them being . . . *in love*. That couldn't be. Lee must've seen that memory wrong.

I know your secret, Gretchen wanted to say. But she couldn't risk Asa's anger now, especially when she partly deserved it. She needed to know all the facts first. She needed to hear the last of his memories from Lee. Then she'd decide what to do.

Asa retracted his legs, bunching them to his chest, and motioned for Gretchen to walk past. She thought it was a trick. She felt sure Asa would try to scare her, or grab at her still-tender ankle, and her feet prickled in anticipation. But Asa did none of those things. He really let her pass. Gretchen did not acknowledge this, or Asa, at all. She walked on, head held high, toward her bedroom.

"Ten bucks says Jolene quits before the gala."

Gretchen stopped, turned, looked at her brother. Was Asa attempting to joke with her?

"Uh . . . yeah," she said through confusion. "Gram's worse than usual this year."

Asa smiled. Not a wrong smile, just a smile.

Gretchen took a deep breath. Then, against her better judgment, she returned to where Asa lay, and took a seat beside him.

"Too bad *we* can't quit," she said.

The faint guitar shrieks coming from Asa's headphones cut out.

"Yeah," he said. "Too bad. We're stuck being Whipples."

"Asa. What you said . . . about us being cursed. About people dying because of us. What did you mean by that?"

Asa bit at some spare skin hanging from his thumb. "Nothing. Just trying to scare you."

"No, you meant it," Gretchen insisted. "Do you know real people who've died? Because of summoners? Because of Rites?"

"Give it a rest, Gretch," Asa groaned. "You and your stupid hypotheticals. If I were you, I'd be worried about real problems. Like . . . wild dogs on the loose."

Gretchen turned red, guilt stinging her chest again.

"I warned you," said Asa. "A Wishing Stone does what it wants, it only causes trouble."

"It didn't cause trouble for me," Gretchen protested. "I meant for it to mess up the house. And anyway, it's not like anyone got hurt."

Asa looked up sharply. He laughed one short laugh. "Right. Yeah. No one got hurt."

"I'm sorry I used it," said Gretchen, "but I had a good reason."

"Whatever. It's gone now, isn't it?"

Gretchen nodded.

"Then good. It's for the best."

"Jolene, where are the crates? Jolene. JOLENE."

Gram's shrill soprano echoed down the hallway, and Gretchen and Asa exchanged a quick look.

"Later," said Asa.

"Yeah," said Gretchen.

When she was safe inside her bedroom, Gretchen reflected on what had just passed. Asa had talked to her, simply *talked*. Would wonders never cease? Asa almost nice, and the Vickeries her allies. When Gram was the only constant left, it was a topsy-turvy world indeed.

33

FELIX

FELIX DID NOT move yet, though he'd seen the lantern flick on and heard the creak of the west end's screen door. He waited for a good hour, until after he had washed and put away the dishes from supper, and after his father had gone back to the examination room with Death to look over the most recently dried herbs.

It was Thanksgiving, according to the calendar Lee had brought back from Boone Ridge Middle at the start of the school year. There, on the fourth Thursday of November, in small red print, read the words *Thanksgiving Day*. In the world at large, these two red words meant something. But in the east end of Poplar House, November's fourth Thursday was another ordinary day.

"It's for people with large families," Vince had told Felix one year, when he had been younger and silly enough to ask his father a question like *Why don't we celebrate Thanksgiving?*

Felix had accepted his father's explanation and left it alone, even long after he found out that people with the smallest of families still ate turkey and cranberry sauce and watched parades on television. This hadn't bothered Felix much. What bothered him was that just a wall away, at the west end of Poplar House, his mother and brother *did* celebrate Thanksgiving. It wasn't a feast, Lee had assured Felix—just a well-salted country ham, a green bean casserole, and a pecan pie. This week, Felix had watched as Lee brought back the groceries from town, stooped from the weight of the sagging paper bags.

Felix and his father did not eat food from the grocery store. The contents of their vegetable stews came from the back garden, and Vince's cured patients often brought basketfuls of homemade food during the holiday season. All in all, these patients were good cooks, but no food of theirs compared to Judith Vickery's. Every Thanksgiving night, Lee would bring out a hearty slice of his mother's pecan pie for Felix to eat. Every night, that is, until this one. Felix still hadn't spoken to Lee, or met him in the usual way, in the conservatory. And if there was no meeting, there would be no pie.

Felix regretted the way he'd pushed Lee away, hiding his feelings. He hadn't meant to go so long without speaking. Only, with every passing day, it grew harder to even think of opening his mouth. Shame welled inside of Felix—the shame of his punishment, and of keeping his brother out for so long, when Lee was the only one who could really understand. But today was Thanksgiving, a time for family, and tonight could be a night for setting things right.

Felix went out to the conservatory, where Lee was sitting, reading a thick book propped on his knees. A rotting board creaked under Felix's shoe, and Lee looked up.

"What do you want?" he asked—his first words to Felix in over two weeks, and less than friendly.

Felix said, "To talk again."

They looked at each other in silence. November wind pressed against the conservatory glass, dragging out mournful creaks.

"Did he lock you down there?" Lee asked in a small voice. Felix nodded, and Lee said, "I'm sorry. It's all my fault."

Felix shook his head. "I chose to follow you. It's not your fault, and I shouldn't have made you feel like it was."

Lee looked at the book in his lap. Felix was close enough now to see the cover.

He'd seen this book once before, in the Whipple library, locked behind glass. What he did not know was how Lee had managed to get his hands on it. Something cracked between Felix's ribs—a quick, breath-punching pain. He and Lee had not spoken for days, and that quickly, he knew nothing of his brother's life.

"Gretchen and I got it," said Lee.

Felix didn't speak right away. "Before," he said, "I didn't think we could do anything about the Agreement."

"And now?"

Felix glanced nervously at the house's east end. "We shouldn't talk about it here."

Lee closed the book, and the boys walked into the wood, a good five-minute hike toward town. Lee was silent, clutching the Book of Rites to his chest beneath his winter coat and breathing heavily into his scarf. Felix stopped under a maple tree. Even after the first snow of the season, its leaves clung stubbornly to their branches, blood red from the strain. Lee was staring at Felix with a new expression—curious, or maybe excited, and that made Felix more nervous about what he had to say.

"If you and Gretchen Whipple think there's really a way to break the Agreement, then I want to try it."

Lee's eyes shone. "You mean it?"

Felix nodded. "I've been thinking about it. A lot."

"Me too. But now that you're finally on my side . . ."

The spot between Felix's ribs cracked wider. "I wasn't ever *not* on your side. I just didn't want you to get hurt. Messing around with the Agreement is dangerous." He heard the sizzle of a single red candle going out—a reminder of Death's punishment. "Really dangerous."

Felix grabbed at the lowest-hanging maple leaf. He broke it off and twirled the stem between his fingers. "I'm tired of watching people die. I'm thirteen. I shouldn't have to watch people die every day."

"You have it tougher than me," Lee said abruptly. "It's worse for you, living with Death."

A short stillness fell on the brothers. Felix looked at Lee, and Lee at him—a silent acknowledgment of a truth they had always known.

"That's not your fault," Felix said.

"I know, but I still feel bad about it."

Felix took a deep breath. "Don't. Tell me what you've been doing with Gretchen instead."

Lee slipped the book out from under his coat. The gold-leaf title gleamed, and though Felix was expecting them, the words rattled his insides all the same: *Book of Rites.*

"I've got a lot to catch you up on." Lee held the Book of Rites toward Felix. "Gretchen and I, um . . . *borrowed* this. I stayed up all night reading it. We're meeting up at school tonight to decide what to do next."

"Which is what?"

Lee said, "We'd better sit down for this." So the brothers settled upon the frost-hardened ground.

"It's not just Rites in here, see," said Lee, flipping to the book's first pages. "There's history. Stories about the summoners and what they used to do. And stories about Shades, too."

Lee ran his finger down the page, along two columns of small text. Felix looked at the headings, scrawled in green ink, each signaling the start of a new story:

MEMORY'S WORK AT THE FIRST BOONE
RIDGE ORPHANAGE, 1801

THE WHIPPLES TAKE OFFICE

INDUSTRY—THE FEATHERSTONE CANNERY OPENS

"A history of Boone Ridge," Felix whispered.

"There's stuff in here I didn't know about. Summoners aren't always bad people, Felix. They aren't supposed to just rule towns and make deals that get them rich. They've got a purpose. A good one, like

Gretchen said. They're supposed to look out for their towns and keep the people safe. There are rules about how Shades can behave, to keep them from getting out of control, and summoners are the ones who enforce those rules. At least, they're supposed to. Look at this."

Lee touched a heading that read *Death and the War Plague.* "Way back during the War of 1812, there was an epidemic in town. It wiped out a whole fourth of the population here in Boone Ridge. We studied it in school. But the book says things our teacher didn't tell us. It says the epidemic wasn't because of poor sanitation or a muggy summer; it's because Death got *out of control.* He started killing people whose time wasn't up yet, taking them for the fun of it. That's when Mayor Whipple—an *old* Mayor Whipple, I guess Gretchen's great-something-grandfather— stepped in. He did something called a Trial Rite. According to this, it's the most important Rite a summoner can do. It calls forward all three Shades when one of them has broken the rules. Then the Shade who's broken the rules is put on trial by the summoner, while the other two Shades sit in judgment. So back then, the old Mayor Whipple did the Rite, and he and Passion and Memory banished that Death from Boone Ridge.

Then another Death came to fill his shoes, and the 'epidemic' ended. Everything went back to normal."

Lee flipped the pages and pointed to another heading: *The Incident of 1922.*

"Or here, when the mining towns near us weren't official towns yet, and the Memory of Boone Ridge was in charge of them. She stole the miners' memories and left them walking around with major amnesia, just because she didn't like how dirty the town had gotten. Those men couldn't even remember the names of their wives or children. People said it was because of too little oxygen way down there in the mines, but the Mayor Whipple back then knew the truth. He did a Trial Rite and Death and Passion banished Memory, and a new Memory—*my* Memory—took her place. Everything was set right, like it was supposed to be. Because that's the Whipples' real job: They protect the town; they keep everything balanced, keep power in check."

Lee flipped forward to a page of only one column of text. The rest of the page was blank. "But look at this. The entries? They stop here, in 1998. Something changed then. Or some*one.* Gretchen's dad, maybe. I think the Whipples forgot what their job was. Maybe they decided to forget on purpose. All the money and power, the good marriages and long lives—maybe those corrupted them, and they couldn't be good, fair summoners anymore. Whatever the reason, the Whipples aren't doing their job."

Through all of this, Felix had remained quiet, thoughtful. Now, the suspicion that had been welling inside him burst: "What happened with Mom and Dad—the Agreement—do you think that was Death and Memory breaking the rules?"

"I don't know," said Lee. "But if it was, there wasn't a good Whipple around to punish them. Who knows what bad things the Shades have been doing since 1998. If they've been acting wrong, then a Whipple's got a right to put them on trial, but if the Whipples have been *letting* all the bad stuff happen in the first place . . . well."

Lee flipped the pages once more. The text in this part of the book was arranged differently, not in columns, but spaced wide apart, in short lines, like poems. At the start of each poem was a title, painted in spindly gold. Between each title and poem was a short list—ingredients and instructions, as though from a cookbook. Rites. And Lee had stopped at the page marked *Trial Rite.*

Felix felt chilled to the muscle. He flipped up the patch from his right eye and looked around, gripped by a sudden fear. If Death were to hear so much as a whisper about this . . .

Lee guessed his brother's thoughts and grabbed his hand, reassuring. "We won't let him find out. You know what this means, right? If we can get the other two Shades to banish Death, then it says here all his deals will be null and void. Which means—"

"Death can't enforce the Agreement," said Felix. "So . . . the Agreement will be broken."

Lee's breaths were quick with excitement, but Felix wasn't smiling. He didn't feel safe yet. "You really trust Gretchen with all this information?"

Felix noted that Lee's cheeks were quite suddenly rosy. "I really think she's on our side," Lee said. "We need a Whipple right now. And I think . . . I think we can help her, too. She needs stuff from us she couldn't get otherwise."

"Dad would be so angry if he knew we were talking to her."

"Mom too. But they don't know Gretchen. And they don't know what this book says. I think if they did, they'd understand."

Felix thought of Death, skulking outside his bedroom window in the pouring rain. Death, holding his iron pincers above the heart of a sickly old miner.

He thought of what his father had said the night before: *I'm a bad man.*

He thought of the cellar.

"Let's do it," Felix said. "Whatever needs to be done."

Lee's grin got bigger. This time, Felix smiled back.

"Oh!" said Lee. "Hang on. I almost forgot."

He fished a foil-covered lump from his coat and placed it in Felix's hand. Felix peeled back the foil, and with it came a sticky coating of cinnamon and crumbled pecans.

"I was going to leave it at the back door," said Lee. "Now I guess I don't have to."

The Vickery twins would be sharing their Thanksgiving pie after all.

34
LEE

Gretchen was waiting for him on the bleachers. From across the field, she was just a smudge of a purple puffer coat and a matching fleece hat.

Lee was late. He'd tried running, but he'd gotten sick after only a minute and had to stop and hold his stomach, sure he would puke at any moment. Even now, he was nauseated, and his head felt light, as though half of it simply wasn't there. They were side effects from absorbing the memories, he knew. He'd thought the symptoms had worn off, but tonight they were worse than ever, slowing his steps as he walked onto the field.

He wished Gretchen hadn't chosen to sit at the very top bleacher. The climb was dizzying, and just as Lee reached her, he stumbled, flailing out of balance and toppling toward her. Gretchen shrieked but threw out her arms, catching Lee's fall.

"Okay?" Her lips brushed the question into his cheek, which Lee was sure had been an accident, because immediately after, Gretchen let go of him completely, and Lee struggled to find his footing and sit down.

Gretchen smirked. "What're you trying to do, Vickery, kiss me?"

"*What?*"

Lee hoped the darkness hid his blistering blush. Emma may have held his hand under the orange table once, but no girl had ever pressed her lips to his cheek—which was almost the same as kissing and was completely Gretchen's fault, which Lee felt very much like pointing out to her. Before he could, light burst into his eyes, and he yelped. Gretchen had turned on a flashlight and was shining it directly in his face.

So much for hiding that blush.

"You don't look so good," said Gretchen.

"I don't feel so good."

"Stomach bug or something?"

"It's the memories."

Gretchen perked up. "Tell me everything."

"I already have."

"But you said there was another memory! Why haven't you looked at it yet?"

"It's not that easy," said Lee, clutching his head. "If I do, I think I'll be puking everywhere. Looking at those memories is kind of like, I don't know, riding a really twisty rollercoaster a hundred times in a row."

"Ick," said Gretchen, looking a little bit sympathetic. "But think of it as a sacrifice for the cause. That memory might contain all the information we need. It could confirm our theory."

"And what's our theory?"

"That Asa and Essie were friends." Gretchen seemed to struggle getting those words out. "That . . . they did that Wishing Stone Rite together. *Why* they did it . . . well, that's what we're still trying to figure out. But Death got mad about something they did, and—and—"

"Killed Essie," said Lee, softly.

"Yeah. That."

Lee didn't blame Gretchen for looking queasy herself. Maybe they were on to why Essie Hasting had died, but that didn't make her alive again. Nothing ever would.

"I'll look at the memory," he said. "Soon. But for now, I've got other important news."

Lee pulled the Book of Rites from his satchel and set it on his lap. Gretchen shone her flashlight beam on the cover. "It looks beat-up," she said.

"It's always looked like that."

"Hm." Gretchen touched the book, contemplative. "And? I assume you've already snooped through it all, so what did you find?"

This was it: the chance to tell her everything. Only, Lee's stomach was molten lava and his mind an arid plain. He closed his eyes and breathed out of his nose. Then, he told Gretchen what he had discovered—about Shades and Whipples and history and, most important, the Trial Rite. When he was through, Gretchen promptly took the book and flipped through its pages. She read over the Trial Rite, silent. Then she said, "We put Death on trial."

"Exactly," said Lee.

"Though really, based on everything you've told me, I guess we could put *all* the Shades on trial. Passion throwing your parents together like that, as a joke, and Memory threatening to take away your father's memories. That all sounds suspect. But Death's the one we'll go after. He's the worst. Making the Agreement, locking Felix in the cellar, killing Essie—and we still don't know *why* he did that—all of that's out of line if ever there was a line to be out of. Well. Don't you think?"

Lee nodded, but he was giving Gretchen a funny look. "You heard what I said about your family, right? They've let all this stuff happen. Aren't you . . ."

Gretchen frowned. "Aren't I what?"

"Well. Angry at me for saying so?"

"I'm mad at you for making me use my bad elbow to catch you," said Gretchen, touching her arm and wincing. "But not about the other stuff. That's not your fault. Anyway, why should I be angry if it's the truth? So my dad isn't doing his job; I've guessed that since I heard him talking to Sheriff Moser and the coroner."

Lee wasn't sure if he should feel relieved or sad. Gretchen didn't wait for him to be either.

"Death," she said. "You agree, right? We put Death on trial."

Lee nodded. "And if Death is banished, that means the Agreement is null and void. That's what the book says. Felix and I figured it all out."

"Felix, huh? You brought him into this?"

"Believe it or not, he's on your side now."

Gretchen snorted. "Is he?"

"Don't look that way."

"What way?"

"Like you want to punch Felix in the face."

"Fine." Gretchen shrugged. "It *does* make it easier for us to do the Rite. Did you see what it calls for?"

Lee recited the ingredients: "A memory, a flower, and a burning candle. Something from each of the Shades."

"Right. So Felix can nab a candle, you can sneak away another memory, and I . . . well . . . what do you know about Passion?"

"You mean, the Shade?"

"*Duh*," said Gretchen, and Lee wasn't sure why he was hot in the face. "We've got to find out where Ms. Hasting lives and steal a flower. What kind of flower is it, anyway? A rose, or—"

"No, it's not like any flower I've seen. In the memory it was purple, with these big, fat petals."

Gretchen looked, thoughtful.

"I don't know how I feel about stealing from Ms. Hasting," said Lee. "I mean, Essie did just die, and . . . well, I know we'd technically be stealing from Passion, but—"

"Hold on. A *purple* flower?"

"Yeah."

Gretchen closed the book. She turned the flashlight back on Lee's face.

"Ow, what—"

"Give me three days."

"What?"

"Three days. I have an idea. And you need to look into that last memory of yours. Soon, okay?"

"Okay."

"Then all right. We reconvene in three days. You

with another memory and Felix with his candle, and me—let's hope—with that flower."

"But, Gretchen—"

"But, Gretchen, *what?*"

This was the part of their meeting that Lee had been looking forward to least.

"You're . . . not the firstborn."

Gretchen's nose crinkled. "So?"

"So . . ." Lee trailed off, the weight of the age-old rule hanging over them both.

"Who else am I going to ask, Lee?" Gretchen burst out. "My dad? *Asa?* No way."

"Yeah, but if you can't do the Rite, then—"

"I can!" Gretchen said. "I *know* I can, if I just get the chance. What, don't you have any faith in me, Vickery?"

Lee felt talked down to, so he stood and said, "You almost got me killed, remember?"

"Once." Then Gretchen smiled a little. "Just once."

Lee sighed. "Three days?"

"Three days." Gretchen handed back the Book of Rites. "You have to keep this. No way I'm gonna risk anyone at home figuring out I stole it. Why are you looking at me like that?"

Lee sighed. "I feel weird having it at home. I'm worried Death or Memory will find it. That maybe they can, I dunno, sniff it out."

"They haven't sniffed it out yet, have they?"

"Well, no, but—"

"Three days. It's not too long. Same time, same place. Deal?"

Lee wasn't sure why he'd tried to argue with Gretchen. There was no point. "Deal."

He expected Gretchen to leave then, but she remained, squinting at him. "Vickery," she said at length. "Do you ever wonder why we're supposed to be enemies? I mean, what's the real point? 'Cause it sure seems like we can do a lot more when we're working together."

Lee nodded. "Maybe the Shades know that."

"Yeah, maybe. Or maybe we humans are just too stupid to get along."

Gretchen sighed, got to her feet, and stomped down the bleachers. Then she stopped and turned to Lee. Her flashlight lit up her face. It could've looked ghastly, but actually, Gretchen Whipple was very pretty in harsh light. Her dark hair spun out from her, tangling in the wind. Her ruby lips were smiling.

"I'm excited, Vickery." She was no longer all business. The way she spoke now, Lee could almost imagine she was an ordinary girl from school. A girl who might be his friend. Or even . . . something more.

"I think this could be it," she said. "I think we're about to solve everything."

"I hope so," said Lee, and Gretchen turned to leave. But when she reached the field, Lee couldn't help himself. "Gretchen!"

She turned once more. "Hm?"

"Did you, uh, *want* me to kiss you?"

Gretchen laughed. The laughs tumbled over each other, loud and crystalline, and at last they stopped, and Gretchen said, "What a stupid thing to ask."

She turned and left him in the dark, alone with his thoughts and the Book of Rites.

Three days.

Three days to open the last of his violet-ribboned jars.

35
FELIX

FELIX STOOD ON the cellar stairs, a red wax candle in hand. It was against everything he had been taught, to steal a candle from Death's collection. But then, what Lee and Gretchen were doing for the Trial Rite was dangerous too. Lee had stolen memories from his mother's collection. Gretchen was doing her own work in town, on the hunt for Passion's flower. If they were going to break the Agreement, all three of them had to pull their weight. Felix reminded himself of this now, as he clutched the stolen candle.

Felix knew that no ordinary force like wind or breath could blow out the flame. It would only go out when Death took its corresponding life. Still, he held the candle with care, afraid he might stumble on his way up the stairs, or that he would get caught, despite his careful planning to slip into the cellar while Death and Vince were busy with a patient in the examination room.

Felix was supposed to be stirring a concoction of herbs and beet broth in the kitchen. He didn't have much time to sneak the candle into his room and hurry back to the stove as though nothing odd had occurred.

Felix did not have time to doubt.

Yet here he was, paralyzed on the cellar stairs, staring at the flame of not just a red wax candle but of a *life*—a resident of Boone Ridge that could be one of Lee's teachers or the man who'd served Felix fried pickles at Creek Diner or even Gretchen Whipple herself.

"Don't think about that," Felix told himself. "Just *go*."

And to his relief, his feet obeyed, leading him up the creaky stairs. He fit the candle into the waiting candleholder he'd placed in the corner of his bedroom, its presence hidden by a tall armoire.

Here he would keep the candle hidden for two more days. Here it would burn until Sunday night, when he, Lee, and Gretchen would meet.

Just two days, Felix thought. *Two days is nothing compared to the rest of your life.*

He hurried into the kitchen, where the beet broth was already gurgling. He stirred its contents, and with every *slosh*, he reassured himself: *Just two more days.*

36
GRETCHEN

IT WAS SATURDAY, the night of the annual Christmas gala, and the atrium of Whipple House was draped in lights, wreaths, and *chiffon* garlands. The smell of mulled cider and pumpkin pies wafted from the kitchen. Somewhere in the house, a harpist was practicing arpeggios. Gram was in the hallway, yelling with unadulterated vehemence at poor Jolene. The door to Mayor Whipple's office was shut—he wouldn't emerge until five minutes before the gala, when he would straighten his bow tie and extend his diplomatic arms to the early arrivals. And Asa was in the backyard, behind the shed, smoking. Gretchen could see the glow of his cigarette from the parlor windows.

This was the moment Gretchen had been waiting for—one of the rare occasions her brother was not holed up in his room, blasting music. Now was the time to act on her suspicions. Gretchen crept toward the back stairs, her toes barely touching the steps as she swept upward and straight for Asa's bedroom. The fluorescent signs taped to his door may have warned dire consequences for anyone who trespassed, but Gram refused to let either of the Whipple children have locks on their doors. So Gretchen ignored the ominous order to KEEP OUT and pushed inside.

Black curtains were drawn over the windows, which forced Gretchen to flip on the overhead light. Band posters covered the walls, their subjects invariably muscled and angry-faced. What Gretchen found surprising was that the room was so *clean*. The bed was made, the dresser and desk dusted. There was no trash or dirty clothes on the floor. All was ordered and put away. Gretchen wasn't sure why she'd assumed Asa's room was a wreck; it had simply fit her idea of him. But she couldn't think about that now.

The flower.

She scanned the room—bed, dresser, computer, speakers, books—but there was not even a glint of purple. Gretchen opened the closet and, standing atop Asa's desk chair, searched its top shelves. Nothing. She checked all the desk drawers, the nightstand, under the bed. No flower. A whispering panic rose in Gretchen's stomach. Maybe she had not seen right on the day of the burial. Maybe the flower in Asa's jacket pocket had not come from Essie. Maybe she had only remembered what she wanted to remember.

Then she fixed on it: the windowsill. She pulled back the heavy, black curtain from the window nearest Asa's bed. There, hidden from view, was a thin, porcelain vase, and in that vase was a violet flower, with large, thick petals, opened mid-bloom.

Very suddenly, everything Gretchen had doubted till now seemed possible: that Essie Hasting could love someone like Asa. That Asa could love anyone at all.

Of course, she thought. *Of course the memories are true.*

Gretchen looked down at Asa, still smoking by the shed. He tugged the cigarette from his lips and tilted his head up, staring at the bedroom window, directly at Gretchen. She gasped, realizing her mistake: She'd let out the light of the bedroom onto the darkening lawn below.

And Asa had seen her.

Gretchen watched in horror as Asa threw down his cigarette and went running for the house. She grabbed the flower from its vase and flew from the room, down the front staircase—another misstep. Asa had not taken the back stairs, like Gretchen expected. He caught her on the landing.

"What do you think you're doing with that?" he growled.

"Asa, please. I know what it is, and I *need* it." She tried to move past him, but Asa blocked her path.

"Need it for what?"

"I—I—" Gretchen's mind puttered and stopped, incapable of producing a lie. Instead, she spat out the truth in one big glop: "I stole the Book of Rites. That's what I used the Wishing Stone for. And now I'm going to do a Trial Rite, and it's going to make everything better."

For one moment, Asa was speechless. Then he began to laugh, low and dark. "In case you didn't realize, there are things you need for that Rite you can't get. And even if you had them, who's the firstborn here?"

"But I *do* have what I need! The Vickeries are helping me, they're getting the other ingredients. And maybe I can do Rites, you don't know. I've got to try. It's the only way to free them. It's the only way to punish Death for . . . for what he did to Essie."

Asa's face turned rigid, but his eyes were aflame. "What did you say?"

"I know, Asa," said Gretchen. "About you and Essie.

That's why you have Passion's flower, right? She gave it to you. You wore it to her burial, I remember."

"You don't know what you're talking about." Asa's words cut the air like sharpened knives, but Gretchen was no longer afraid.

"I do know. You and Dad can keep all the secrets you want, but I *know what I'm talking about.*"

"You don't know the truth!" shouted Asa. "Dad hasn't told you the things he's told me."

"Then *you* tell me!" Gretchen shouted back.

"Fine," said Asa, fiercely. "You want to know the whole truth? Then here it is: Dad made a deal with Death. Not the usual deal, for the good of Boone Ridge or anyone else. He asked to live *forever.* And Death said Dad could break the rules, but only if Death could break rules, too. So Dad lets him. He lets Death do whatever he wants."

Gretchen's throat felt strangely sticky. "Just so he can live . . . forever?"

"He told me, my sixteenth birthday. And you know what? I didn't care. I was fine, same as him, letting Death do whatever he wanted to this town. So it's my fault. It's my fault Essie's dead." Asa's voice broke on the final words, and Gretchen felt suddenly weak.

"That's . . . not true," she whispered. "How could that be your fault?"

"It is. And if you keep messing with this, with those Vickeries, you're going to get yourself killed, too. And it's got to stop, Gretch. It's got to stop for good."

"Where are you going?" cried Gretchen. Asa was taking the stairs three at time, and then he was out the front door. Before Gretchen reached the porch, she heard the roar of Asa's motorbike. She watched, helpless, as he sped from the driveway.

And then she realized—she knew where Asa was heading.

Gretchen thought of the Christmas gala, the bustle and buzz in the house. Gram would ground her for all eternity, ship her to boarding school. But Gretchen had no choice: she had to chase down Asa. And so she set off, running as hard as she could, toward the house in Poplar Wood.

The wind whipped against Gretchen's skin, cold and biting. She should've thought to wear a coat, a scarf, a hat. But Gretchen wasn't thinking of warmth; she was thinking of speed. How soon could she get to the wood and stop whatever Asa planned to do? Was he going to yell at the brothers? Vandalize their house, like Gretchen had before?

Asa was going to ruin Gretchen's perfect plan with Lee and Felix, all she had worked on for weeks. She had to stop him. But how could she ever run faster than a motorbike?

You can, though, shouted an electric thought. *You can if you take the shortest route and he goes the long way around.*

Yes. Gretchen remembered now, from her ride with Asa back from the Poplar Wood: He had taken the long way, avoiding Hickory Park.

Because of Essie, Gretchen thought. *Because of what happened that night. All the bad memories, all the bad feelings inside.*

Gretchen's fingers curled around the purple flower in her hand, shielding it from the wind and cold. She ran toward Hickory Park and the wood beyond it. She didn't stop once, crossing streets, ignoring the indignant honks of cars. Her throat burned while the world around her darkened from dusk to night.

Run, she ordered her legs. *Run, beat him there.*

Her sprained ankle cried out in protest, but Gretchen ignored the pain. Her vision clouded with something white, whipping about in powdery flurries. It was snowing again. Gretchen ran harder, through the wintry swell, her feet hitting concrete, then asphalt, and finally, earth. She'd reached the edge of Poplar Wood.

Gretchen stopped for only a moment, to bend and catch some breath. That's when she saw it, leaned against a nearby hickory tree—Asa's bike, dismounted and abandoned.

"No," Gretchen heaved out. "*No!*"

And she was running again, into the wood, into the dark, straining her eyes to see past snow and branches.

"Lee!" she shouted. "Felix! ASA!"

As always, the trees did not answer. Only the wind blew back.

"Asa, please! Stop! Where are you? Asa, please, just wait!"

Then she saw it, ahead—a black-blue silhouette against the light of house windows. Asa was only yards away from the house in Poplar Wood. He was standing still, his shoulders hunched, face turned toward something on the ground.

"Asa!" Gretchen called, not sure why she was filled with such sudden dread.

Asa did not respond. He knelt to the ground to pick up an object from the grass. Gretchen drew closer, breathing hard, trying to see. Something dark and thin was slithering up Asa's arm, beneath the sleeve of his shirt, and toward his chest. Slithering . . . like a snake.

"Asa!" Gretchen shouted again, coming up on him. "What are you—what is that?"

At last, Asa looked up. There was a strange light in his eyes, and movement beneath his shirt—a slight bulge just above his heart. Gretchen thought she saw a flash of yellow. Then a pained look crossed Asa's face, only for an instant. He slipped his hand into his shirt, in the space between buttons.

"It's fine now," he said, his words tissue-thin. "It found me again. It's given me what I wish."

Asa removed his hand from his shirt. It was covered in liquid, shimmering and red. Blood. And in the palm of his hand rested an object, small and dark like coal.

It was the Wishing Stone.

37

LEE

IT MIGHT BE NOTHING.

Lee sat at the end of his bed, the unopened jar in his hands. This last memory might be about Essie. It could be the final answer Gretchen Whipple was after. An answer that, if Lee was honest, *he* was after now: Why, exactly, had Death killed Essie Hasting?

Or it could be nothing, he reminded himself.

Lee was going to find out. He had already snuck another jar from the canning room for the Trial Rite—this one a green-ribboned jar of a clear, happy memory labeled *Remember*. Lee had first planned to take a memory marked *Forget*. It would have been better, nobler of him, perhaps. But the thought of opening another memory best left forgotten was more than he could stomach.

Lee had stored away that stolen memory for the Trial Rite. But now was the time to open another jar—the last of the dark memories. This was the part of the deal he dreaded most, the part that had given him bad dreams the night before and an ache that gnawed so fiercely at his stomach that not even his favorite sweet potato casserole sounded appetizing now.

The memories were affecting him. They were bad for him—maybe even worse than he knew. But he'd made a deal with Gretchen and Felix, and this was his end of it. If he could do this one thing, maybe they would break the curse on this house.

Lee unscrewed the lid. He ducked his head toward the open jar and breathed in. This time, he felt the memory flooding his senses, wrapping them in a hot, waxy substance that drew him into another place and time.

He closed his eyes.

He opened them.

He was standing outside, drenched in a deluge of rain. His clothes were soaked, hands pruny. Thunder clapped, and a sizzle of lightning cracked through the sky, lighting the surrounding trees.

He was in Hickory Park.

"Asa!"

A girl was running toward him, mascara bleeding down her face, into the corners of her mouth.

"Asa!" Essie shouted again, catching his hand.

He said, "I thought you'd changed your mind."

"What? It's just a little bit of rain!" Essie shouted over a roar of thunder. He could see the kindness in her face, even through the storm. "We said we'd do it tonight, so we're doing it tonight."

"We still don't know what's going to happen," he said. "Maybe those other summoners gave you the wrong Rite."

"The Rite isn't wrong, and you know it. We have to start somewhere, and if a Wishing Stone can give you anything, it will give us what we wish: for things to be right again."

He felt afraid, though he would never admit it. He felt excited, too. And there was another feeling that boiled in his gut. It was a terrible aching, and it had everything to do with Essie.

"Blood first," she said. "Like the book says."

He stooped to where his soggy backpack lay. From it, he removed a dagger. Its hilt was made of bronze, inlaid with opals that exploded in color each time another wave of lightning broke across the sky. Essie took the dagger from him, and before he could speak, she'd sliced it across her open palm. Then she handed the dagger back, and he cut his own hand. Pain pinched down his nerves as hot blood emerged.

"Now," said Essie, leading him across damp grass to a gaping gray expanse. They stood on the edge of the cliff in Hickory Park. Essie took his hand, and he squeezed hers. Their hot blood pooled together and dripped down, into the ravine below.

Commingled blood, dropped from a great height. That is what the Rite had called for, and that is what they had provided. Now all that remained was the poem.

"Say it loud," said Essie, placing the notebook in his clean hand. The rain fell hard, but he could still make out the title of the page: *Wishing Rite*. He knew the poem he had to read. Only he, the summoner, could do this.

"Oh Death!" he shouted into the storm. "We implore thee, Darkest Shade, to grant us what fate first forbade."

The summoner knew the words that followed, but his throat had closed; his mouth was sealed up.

Then there was warmth on his wrist. Essie's.

"You can do it," she whispered. "I know you can."

His throat opened. His mouth unstuck. He continued.

> *"Bestow on us the Wishing Stone,*
> *that makes all hidden mysteries known.*
> *Reveal yourself to summoning eyes, and*
> *give to us the sacred prize!"*

The storm ceased. In an instant, the rain was swallowed back into the sky. The thunder collapsed upon itself, folding into silence. All was still in Hickory Park, save for the drip-dripping of water from branches.

Essie turned to him. "Did it work?" she whispered. "Where is he?"

A voice said, "Here."

They turned together. Standing between two sturdy hickory trees was a man dressed in a fine black suit. He wore a white bow tie and a silk top hat, and he looked at them with a cool expression, no trace of a smile or frown on his handsome features.

"Who has summoned me?" Death asked. "You, young Whipple?"

"I—I request the Wishing Stone."

"Do you, indeed?" Death's voice was rich, but it paused in strange places. "For what purpose do you desire such a precious gift?"

A thought flashed in the summoner's mind—only

hotter and stronger than a mere thought. A desire. One word: freedom.

"We want to be free," said Essie, stepping beside him and slipping her hand into his. "Asa from his summoning, and me from my apprenticing. We've had enough. We're sixteen, and we know our own minds. We don't want to be trapped the way our parents were. We want freedom, and the Wishing Stone is going to give us that."

Death's gaze shifted to Essie. His pale lips curled inward—so much so that he appeared to no longer have lips at all.

"You," said Death. "You serve another, one of my enemies."

Essie stood tall, unmoved. "That doesn't matter. A Rite is a Rite. You have to do as we ask."

"Passion doesn't know you're here." Though Death's face remained expressionless, his voice was hungry, intent. "No, you two have done this all on your own. I can see it in your hearts. Yes, I see why you desire the Wishing Stone. I know what you desire, foolish children, and as you say, you summoned me, and you will have your prize."

Something cold and dry suddenly pressed into the summoner's free hand. He looked down to discover he was holding a small dark stone.

"Now." Death turned a cold, apathetic gaze toward Essie. "I have business of my own."

"No," said Essie, stepping back, uncertainty touching her face. "Our business here is done. You've given us the Wishing Stone, and now we part ways."

Death did not seem to hear. "Passion need never know," he said, drawing nearer. "I could make it look like the most human of accidents. No one will say otherwise, least of all your coward father, young Whipple. He will not lift a finger to stop or accuse me."

The summoner stepped in front of Essie, his heart crashing. "Essie hasn't done anything. You can't touch her."

"Hasn't done anything?" Something flashed in Death's blue eyes. Something horrible. "Oh, I beg to differ. She's done plenty. Such an industrious apprentice, I'm sure. Only now, it seems, she's grown tired of the work. Like you, Whipple. You wish to be free—of your family name, your obligations. Well, dear ones, you don't need a Wishing Stone for that. Why don't I help you personally, dear Essie? I can grant you a permanent stop to all your obligations."

"I—" said Essie. "I don't—"

"It's too perfect," said Death, removing evening gloves from his long, bony hands. "I will finally bring as much calamity on Passion as Passion has brought on me."

A blast of icy cold shook through the summoner's chest. He gasped for air but breathed in nothing. A dense, white void began to expand in his mind. As it grew, he became aware of the reason for his discomfort. Death had reached through his chest to where Essie stood behind him and curled his fingers around her neck.

"Asa!" she cried, the word weak and constricted.

"Let this be a lesson, young Whipple!" Death's words were a birdlike shriek. "No matter what plans you make, no matter which Rites you choose, you will never outsmart a Shade!"

"Asa!" Essie gasped, the blood draining from her once-rosy face.

"LEE!"

The cold rushed from Lee's body, and breath returned to his lungs. He blinked against spotty vision and sat up.

"Lee!" the voice shouted again. "Open up, *please!* Hurry!"

He wasn't Asa, the summoner, and it wasn't Essie who was calling his name.

"Gretchen?" he said groggily, crawling across his bed to unlatch the window she'd been knocking against. Gretchen's hair was windblown, and there was terror in her eyes.

"Leander!" Judith called from the parlor. "What on earth is going on back there?"

"It's nothing!" shouted Lee.

His shoulders were shaking—but no, it was Gretchen's hands, shaking his shoulders. In fact, all of Gretchen was shaking violently.

"What is it?" Lee asked, alarmed. "Gretchen, what's wrong?

Gretchen made rasping sounds with her throat, but no words came out.

Lee looked past her, to where his brother stood at the conservatory door.

Felix said, "There's been an accident."

38
FELIX

THE EAST END of Poplar House reeked of blood.

Asa Whipple lay on the examination table, heaving out stuttering breaths. He was bleeding from his chest, a steady stream of thick blood. He needed Vince Vickery's care, but the trouble was, Vince was not at home.

"He's making a house call," Felix explained to Lee, through the open window of the examination room. He pushed up the hair from his sweaty brow, tapping his foot violently on the ground. "A follow-up with one of his patients in Arley Gap. Why did it have to be *now*?"

Gretchen was hunched over Asa's body, pressing a blood-dirtied towel against his stomach. Her hands were stained and her cheeks speckled bright red.

"Felix," she cried, "it won't *stop*."

Felix had done all he could think of in the panic following Gretchen's appearance. He'd helped her drag her brother's body into the house. He'd emptied his father's supply cabinet of gauze and towels and every herb he'd seen Vince use for wound stanching. But something was wrong. Though there was a never-ceasing flow of blood coming from just above Asa's heart, there was no proper wound, no source. It was as though the blood was seeping from the very pores of Asa's skin.

"I don't think I can stop it," Felix said. "It's not an ordinary wound. There's something wrong here. Something very wrong."

Felix clenched his fists, angry with himself. He was Death's apprentice-in-training, wasn't he? What was the point of that—of thirteen years bound to Death—if he couldn't save a life?

A Wishing Stone, that's what Gretchen had said. Asa had held a Wishing Stone, and Gretchen was afraid that, in that moment, his deepest desire had been to die. With each passing minute, Felix felt a horrible suspicion growing. Maybe this was something not even his father could fix. Maybe all anyone could do now was wait until Death appeared in the room. Wait until he approached the foot of the examination table, his metal pincers raised . . .

No.

Felix had to try something, anything else. He took a coral box from one of the medicine shelves and emptied its dried contents into his palm. Rose petals and rosemary. Felix had seen his father use the combination before to revive failing patients. He now pressed a handful to Asa's chalky lips.

Asa coughed, and his eyes flew open. They were bright red—pupil, iris, and all.

From the window, Lee let out a shriek. Felix toppled back. Only Gretchen remained where she was. Her eyes were wide—from fear, Felix thought at first. But then she spoke.

"The Rite," she said, looking to Felix and Lee. "What are we thinking? *We do the Rite now.* I've got Passion's flower here. If we banish Death, then he can't take Asa away."

"I'll get the memory," said Lee. "And the book." He disappeared from the window.

"It's all I can think of," Gretchen said, turning, desperate, to Felix.

But Felix was staring into the darkest corner of the room. Through his unseeing eye, he saw a well-dressed gentleman standing there. Death checked his pocket watch and nodded at Felix cordially.

"Felix?" said Gretchen. "Felix!"

"It's too late," he whispered.

He recognized the look in Death's eyes.

"Here!" shouted Lee, clambering back to the open window and holding out a green-ribboned jar.

"Maybe it is too late," Gretchen said to Felix, "but we've got to at least try."

Felix ran from the room. He skidded into his bedroom and retrieved the red wax candle from its hiding place.

"Felix," Lee shouted. "Felix, hurry! Death's talking, and it doesn't sound good!"

No longer did Felix treat the candle with care. He raced it back to the examination room, its flame flickering wildly.

Lee had placed the Book of Rites on the window ledge, and was holding out a green-ribboned jar. Above it, Gretchen held a purple flower. Felix watched Death, still in the corner, eyeing his pocket watch. He seemed distracted by his job, this impending death. Otherwise, surely, he would've said something about Asa and Gretchen's unwanted presence here. Otherwise, surely, he would have seen what they were attempting to do. He looked as calm as ever. Was it because he was unaware of their plan, or was it simply because he knew it wouldn't work?

"We've got to do it fast," said Gretchen. "Heat the memory with the candle—right, Lee?"

Lee looked up from the open book. "Heat the memory with candle's flames, then take off the lid and add Passion's flower."

"Right," said Gretchen, turning to Felix. "Let's do this."

39

GRETCHEN

SHE FELT THE heat of the candle's flame. Though Felix held it steady, its fire licked toward Gretchen's knuckles, while also warming the memory in Lee's hands. Then, without knowing how, Gretchen *knew*. It was time. She unscrewed the lid of the memory jar and dropped Passion's flower inside.

With watering eyes, Gretchen watched as the petals curled in the liquid. Then nothing remained of the flower, and the liquid memory turned from clear to electric blue. An image flashed in Gretchen's mind— a birthday cake slathered in pink-whipped frosting, a bunch of gold balloons tied to a chair. Gretchen felt a twinge of remorse, uttered a silent *sorry* to whoever's memory she'd taken, never to return. Then the image passed, and all that remained was the blue liquid before her. It was congealing, despite the flame Felix held beneath it.

And again, Gretchen knew: It was time.

She grabbed the Book of Rites from the window ledge, where Lee had placed it. The poem there was only three lines long. Gretchen spoke the words aloud: "*Now convene, oh mighty Shades, whether day or night. Stand witness two against the one, for errant deeds must be set right, till summoning work is done.*"

All was silent.

The Rite settled upon the room.

Gretchen closed her eyes.

When she opened them, she toppled back in shock.

Three figures stood before her. On the left was a woman dressed in a white lace dress. She had flowing light hair, and a circlet of diamonds ran across her throat. Memory.

On the right stood a figure dressed in a scarlet robe, with a sharp jaw and short, curly hair. A smirk switched up Passion's face, as though he or she—Gretchen couldn't say which—had just heard an excellent joke.

And there, in the middle, stood Death, looming over Gretchen like a weather-bent tree. He wore a fine black suit, and his cuff links winked in the red candle's light.

In one hand, he held a silver pocket watch. His gaze resembled a dark and yawning cave.

I did it, Gretchen thought. *Me, a secondborn. I really did it. It really worked.*

Then, Memory spoke. "Why have you brought us here, summoner?" Her voice rang out like clinking crystal. "Who has trespassed against the humans of Boone Ridge?"

Gretchen worked hard to force sound from her mouth. "D-Death. He's the one who's on trial."

"Very young to be summoning," said a playful coo that belonged to Passion. "*Very* young."

"Maybe," said Gretchen, straightening. "But I know what I'm doing, and I know how this works. You and Memory have to stand in judgment of Death for what he's done."

Another voice filled the room, as gentle as a tap upon the shoulder. "Pray tell, what am I supposed to have done?"

Steeling herself, Gretchen faced Death.

"You murdered Essie Hasting," she said. "She and Asa asked for the Wishing Stone to be free of you all. To stop being apprentice and summoner. So you killed Essie. And you *liked* it, too. Because she was Passion's apprentice, and you wanted revenge."

Passion no longer smirked. Fire crackled in their eyes. "Excuse me?"

Death adjusted one of his cuff links, looking magnificently bored. "It's nothing worse than what you did to me, dear Passion. Forcing me to be bound here like a dog with Memory for a companion. We're even, wouldn't you say?"

"*You.*" Passion said like it was a poisonous word.

"Me," Death echoed calmly. "And if you're going to banish me, so be it. It was worth it, to watch your precious apprentice die."

An inhuman scream filled the room, so loud that Gretchen put her hands to her ears. She looked on in horror as Passion raised their fists in the air, mouth gaping in rage. And terrifying as the spectacle was, Gretchen began to hope. It was working. *The Trial Rite was working.*

At the very moment Passion's scream became unbearable, it ceased, replaced by words: "We must banish him. He must pay."

Memory fluttered her long lashes and spoke. "Death, the charges laid against you are that you acted beyond the bounds of your station. You took the life of Essie Hasting, Passion's apprentice, out of vengeance and before her allotted time."

"These are the charges," said Passion, rage-filled eyes fixed on Death. "Memory, how do you find the defendant, Death?"

"Guilty," Memory said, with no hesitation. "Passion, how do you find the defendant, Death?"

"Guilty," said Passion, uttering the word like a curse.

All three Shades of Boone Ridge then turned their eyes upon Gretchen. They were, it seemed, waiting for her to act.

"I—I—" she stammered.

Over the past few days, Gretchen had been convincing herself that she could do the Trial Rite. That her birth order didn't matter, and neither did the fact that she had not been trained. Her mind and determination—that's what would get her through in the end. And they *had*. But Gretchen hadn't thought through what to do if everything went according to plan. What was she supposed to do now? *How* did she banish Death? She looked desperately to Lee, who looked at the Book of Rites and back at Gretchen, shaking his head to say *There's nothing here*.

Gretchen took a steadying breath. She replanted her feet and lifted her chin toward the Shades. If she had summoned them, then she *was* a summoner. It was time to act like one, even if that meant making things up. She thought of what she knew about normal, human trials. The jury or judge declared the defendant innocent or guilty. And if guilty . . . then came the sentencing.

"Death," she said, resolved. "By the . . . um, power vested in me by your fellow Shades, I hereby sentence you to be banished from Boone Ridge, never to return again. And when you leave, all your deals will be null and void . . . and . . . stuff." She winced but kept her chin held high.

Death regarded Gretchen coolly, as though she had merely stepped on his toes.

"Very well, young Whipple," he said. "But your brother's life is still forfeit."

"No, it isn't!" cried Gretchen. "Not if you're banished. Any agreements you had—"

"Oh, but Asa didn't have an agreement. He had a *desire*, born deep from his heart of hearts. You can banish me to the ends of the earth, but I am not the Wishing Stone. Its work cannot be undone. That matter's quite out of my hands. I must merely take the life it's already claimed."

"But—!" Gretchen looked desperately to where Asa lay, prone and damp with blood.

Death drew closer. "Would you like to know an agreement that *will* be broken, though? A little arrangement I made with your father."

He asked to live forever.

Gretchen recalled Asa's words, and as though he could hear them, Death smiled. "You understand, don't you, that if I am banished, Mayor Whipple will eventually die? Would you like to be responsible for killing your own father?"

Gretchen opened her mouth, and shut it. Her father's agreement. She had not thought of that. It was such a new revelation, and there had been no time.

"Don't listen to him!" said a voice behind Death. Felix. "He's trying to trick you. Your father didn't have a right to make that deal, Gretchen. It's natural that everyone dies. You wouldn't be killing him, it's only *natural*."

"SILENCE, BOY." Death turned upon Felix in a furious whirl. "You are a servant. A voiceless set of hands and feet, made to do my bidding. You have no say here!"

It was enough to shake Gretchen from her speechlessness.

"No, *you* shut up!" she shouted at Death. "Leave him alone, you—you *bully*! That's what you are. You might have power, and you might make deals, but at the end of the day you're no better than stupid Emma or Dylan. You're nothing but a bully, and you've bullied long enough. So my dad will die the way he would've without a deal. That's the way it's supposed to be. You don't get to threaten him, or me. You don't get to threaten anyone again. We've banished you, Death. You're no longer welcome here. So *leave*."

Death's rage had vanished. His eyes shone with something Gretchen could not describe.

"I cannot disobey," he said. "But I've one last matter to attend to on my way out: your brother's wish."

He reached into his suit coat and removed a pair of metal pincers.

Gretchen tried to move but found her feet were frozen in place. In horror, she watched as Death opened the pincers and lunged toward Asa's body.

Lee slammed his hands against the sides of the open window, as though the air there were made of glass. "Gretchen!" he shouted.

"ASA!" Gretchen screamed.

There was a flurry of light. Gretchen stumbled as two figures, red and white, pushed past her. Passion gripped Death's left shoulder, Memory his right.

"You've done enough damage here," said Passion. "We will see to the rest."

"No!" shouted Death. "It's my right. It's—"

"You have no rights," said Memory. "We banish you."

A sound ripped through the room, loud and thundering. Gretchen dropped to her knees and clutched her ears, trying to block out the noise. She heard shouts from the others, the rattling of furniture, the clanging of dishes.

Then, silence.

40
FELIX

PAIN BURST IN Felix's right eye.

He screamed. His eye was burning, *burning*. A hand touched his shoulder, but Felix shrugged it away. He sank to the floor, and realized he was no longer screaming but crying.

The pain faded.

Then came the silence.

Felix opened his unseeing eye, and with it he saw— nothing. Nothing at all.

Death was no longer in the examination room.

And Felix knew: Death would not be in this room ever again.

41

GRETCHEN

GRETCHEN PRESSED HER palms against the floorboards and opened her eyes. Asa lay dead still upon the examination table. Passion was leaning over him, brushing hair from his forehead as though he were a child in need of tending. Memory stood close by, looking on in a blinkless gaze.

Then, Asa began to sputter and cough.

"Asa!" Gretchen tore to her feet and raced to his side.

"Huh," he wheezed. "Guess you can do a Rite after all."

"Shut up," Gretchen said happily. "You're okay. You're *okay*."

She pulled away the bloodied cloths from his chest, but there she stopped short. The bleeding had not ceased. Thick red liquid still oozed from Asa's skin.

"What's happening?" Gretchen cried. "Why hasn't it stopped?"

"Death spoke true to you," said Passion, in a gentle drawl. "The work of a Wishing Stone cannot be undone."

"What?" Gretchen looked frantically to Asa's blood-drained face. "No. That can't be right. We did the Rite; we banished Death. It can't work this way. That's not . . . that's not *fair!*"

"My dear," said Passion, "if your brother's deepest desire was for death, then that is what the Wishing Stone will grant him. That wish cannot be un-granted. Your brother's life will linger until a new Death arrives. Then, it will be taken for good."

"NO!" Gretchen slammed her hand on the table. "There must be something you can do! You're *Shades.* You're the keepers of the Wishing Stone. If anyone can make this better, you can. So do it. Make it better. Make it right!"

Memory raised her eyes to Passion's. Over Gretchen's head, they seemed to speak in silent conversation. They turned to Gretchen and, in time with each other, shook their heads.

Gretchen turned to the two Vickery brothers—Lee at the window and Felix on the ground. They looked just as helpless and answerless as she was. "But," she said to the Shades, "he's my brother. He's a *summoner!* Doesn't that mean anything to you?"

Memory looked over Asa's body, her face wrinkled in distaste. "We do not much care for Whipple summoners. Death acted beyond his bounds, but so did your father. Perhaps it would be best to let the Whipple line fade away. Allow a new family of summoners to take their place."

"My desire . . . my desire . . . wasn't for death."

Asa was pale, his breaths shuddering out, shallow and frail, but with effort, he was speaking. He coughed weakly into his fist, staining his knuckles with blood. "What I desired—what I wanted all along . . . I wanted to be free of the Whipple name." Asa pointed a shaking finger to Felix and Lee. "Look at them. They're practically hermits, freaks. But their lives aren't part of a political scheme. Dad got it all wrong. It's the apprentices here who work for our town, not for themselves. Apprentices like—like Essie, who only did what she was asked. Who only wanted to be free. That's what we wanted: just to be free of our histories."

"Asa," said Gretchen. "You never told me that. I never knew."

"Enough of human matters," said Memory, sounding impatient. "Passion, there is no business left for us here."

Gretchen's mind turned over frantically. She gripped the table, her eyes alight with a sudden, searing idea. "Asa!" she cried. "If that's what you most desired, then there's another way. You don't have to *die* to be rid of the Whipple name." She turned toward the Shades. "Don't you see? He doesn't have to die. He could stop being a Whipple. He could be a *Hasting* instead."

Memory pressed a pale hand to her temple, surprised, it seemed, by the sudden suggestion. Passion, however, kept steady eyes on Gretchen. "What are you proposing, young Whipple?"

Gretchen pointed to Passion. "You need a new apprentice now that Essie is gone. But we Whipples already know about you Shades. Asa would be easy to train."

Passion's lips parted, a very slight O. "Are you suggesting that *this boy* would replace my darling apprentice?"

"But he wouldn't be a Whipple anymore, don't you see? Not if he took on the Hasting name. That is"—Gretchen turned to Asa, her eyes wide and pleading—"if . . . if he wanted to."

Asa continued to cough, weak and wheezing, into his hand.

"I know," said Gretchen. "I know it's not what you wanted. You said yourself: The Wishing Stone has its own way of doing things. That things don't always turn out the way you want, that people die. But *you* don't have to die. Not if your deepest desire is to be a Hasting."

She clutched his free hand, prying its bloodied fingers loose to reveal the Wishing Stone. "Wish for that, Asa," she whispered. "Make that your deepest desire. Please."

Asa shut his eyes. He folded the Wishing Stone back into his palm, drawing in rattling breaths.

Gretchen looked up at Passion. "It *can* work that way, can't it?"

Asa had grown very still. Gretchen watched his chest rise and fall, holding in her own breath. Then, to her surprise, Passion reached out and placed a hand across Asa's worn face.

"What!" Gretchen shouted. "What are you doing?"

"Claiming the boy," Passion said.

Gretchen watched as, slowly, Asa's face filled back up with color, turning the same scarlet hue of Passion's robe. Then Passion stepped away. Though the examination table and Gretchen herself were a terrible mess of blood, the mysterious outpouring had stopped. Asa was whole again. Slowly, he pushed himself into a sit. He looked as much alive now as when he'd fought with her on the staircase. In fact, Gretchen thought, he looked more alive than she had ever seen him before.

Gretchen cried out, flinging her arms around him. His body stiffened at her touch, but after a moment, relaxed.

"Why didn't you tell anyone?" Gretchen whispered. "About what happened with Essie? It wasn't your fault."

Asa stiffened once more. "No one would have believed that. No one would have believed *me*. Not even Dad. I think . . . I think he suspected. I think I'm another reason why he covered the whole thing up."

Gretchen wanted to argue, but she wondered if Asa wasn't right after all. The people of Boone Ridge only saw what they wanted to see. How would they understand that Essie Hasting's death had to do with a thirteen-year grudge among Shades, or a terrible deal their mayor had made long ago? How would they understand that Asa—who smiled all wrong and picked fights for fun—had cared for a girl with all his heart?

Gretchen understood her brother, though—maybe not completely, maybe only in very small part. But she knew him better now than she had before. Now, when he was fated to leave her. The full weight of Gretchen's proposal fell upon her: She'd saved Asa's life, but only by bargaining that life away. She'd asked for him to be an *apprentice*, of all things. Panicked, Gretchen pulled away, looking to Passion.

"You claimed him?"

Nodding, Passion said, "His life will do as a substitute. I will train him in the way I once trained Essie under the supervision of her mother, Mrs. Hortense Hasting."

"But . . . you're not taking him right away, are you?"

Gretchen knew but dreaded the answer: Asa would not be picking her up from school again, on his noisy motorbike or in noisier Whipplesnapper. She would never again catch him smoking in the backyard, or hear his stupid rock music blasting through her bedroom wall.

"Gretch." Asa touched her arm. "It's better this way."

Gretchen shook her head. "But I—I didn't think about—"

"You suggested it, but the Wishing Stone wouldn't have changed its course if I didn't change my own mind. And . . . this is for the best. It's the one way I can stay close to Essie. I can honor her memory."

Gretchen's eyes filled with tears. "I'm sorry, Asa. I didn't know. . . . I . . . didn't know."

"And I didn't know my kid sister was so smart." Asa smirked, then turned his eyes to Passion. "I'm ready. Do what you want."

And, for the first time in a long time, one of the Vickery boys spoke.

"You don't know what it's like," said Felix, getting to his feet. "You don't know what you're doing, Asa. It's your whole life—forever."

"I don't really have a choice, kid. That was the deal."

"But!" Felix turned to Memory and Passion, who regarded him impassively. "I know what it's like, to be an apprentice. No one should have to live that way. Not even a Whipple."

"That's touching, kid," said Asa, "but it seems like you had a worse time of it than most. Wasn't that your boss that just got banished?"

Felix said nothing to that.

"I can assure you all," Passion said, "I have nothing but the highest standards for my apprenticeships. And if anyone doubts that—well. I'm sure I'll be held accountable."

Passion turned to Gretchen, and she realized that this last part was directed at her.

"But," she said, "I can still see Asa, can't I? He doesn't have to keep away?"

"You may see him," said Passion. "Though, understand his life belongs to me now. He cannot be the brother to you that he once was. He cannot live in your house or partake in your family's daily rituals. He is no longer a Whipple. No longer a summoner. He is an apprentice. That is *our* Agreement."

With difficulty, Gretchen nodded. "Quid pro quo, huh?"

Gretchen knew Asa wouldn't want another hug. So even though it was the worst possible time to do it, she smiled at him.

"I think I'll actually miss you," she told him.

Asa smiled back, all wrongly. Gretchen did not expect another answer.

"Come," said Passion, offering Asa a hand. "Let us be away."

Asa took the hand, and together he and the red-cloaked Shade stepped into the hallway. Only Gretchen followed them out, watching Asa leave through the conservatory, watching as he and Passion were swallowed into the dark of Poplar Wood.

Then came silence, different from all the silences before it.

Asa was gone.

42
LEE

"LEE," SAID MEMORY.

She had joined him in the conservatory. Lee could see her still, though she seemed more smudged at her edges, as though by eraser. The Rite, he guessed, was wearing off.

"The Agreement is breaking," Memory said. "Can you feel it?"

Lee swallowed. "I—I don't think so."

"You will. A new Death will arrive, seeking out a new apprentice. Your father and brother—they are now free. But you . . ."

Lee understood. "Mother will still work for you. I know. That was never what was wrong. The Agreement's gone, and that's what really matters."

As Lee spoke, his stomach curdled and his vision splotched. He grabbed at the windowsill to steady himself.

"You took in memories," Memory said. "I know. I see them now, in your mind. They will be with you always, child. You will never be quite healed of them. They will haunt your sleep and weaken your body. Is that what you wish for? A life of illness and bad dreams?"

"No," said Lee. "Of course not."

Memory touched his arm. In the lamplight, she was a radiant vision of white.

"I could take it away," she said, her voice a mere whisper. "The sorrow you drank, and all your own bad memories. These many years of living apart from your father. All of that, I would take away. We would work together."

Lee found it difficult to breathe, difficult to think of anything other than Memory's kind face.

"You could sign the contract early, if you'd like." Memory's voice was soothing—an antidote to every stomach pain he'd ever had. "I would allow it, Leander, to alleviate your suffering. You could choose to be my apprentice now."

In that moment, it seemed to Lee that he was standing alone—not in the conservatory, but in a still and formless space, with only Memory for company.

Her words were calming, and Lee wondered: Had his life with her ever been so bad? It was the *Agreement* that was bad, really, and now that was over . . .

All Memory was asking was for him to go on bottling and labeling jars, and to carry out the work his mother did now.

The work his mother had always done.

Forever.

The formless place faded, and in rushed November cold. Lee was in the conservatory again, himself, with a stomachache still, but a clearer mind. He looked up at Memory's kind face and said, "I won't ever be your apprentice."

Memory did not argue. She removed her hand from Lee's shoulder and seemed to nod, once, though Lee was no longer sure of where Memory's head was. She was fading fast, into a blur of white—a hovering cloud, and then . . . nothingness.

All that remained was a voice, which whispered in his left ear: "*Not today, but perhaps . . . later.*"

Then, a familiar sound: a bittersweet melody, hummed low, in the gentlest of tones.

Not today, thought Lee, shaking the song from his head. *Not ever.*

He looked out to the wood and the darkened sky. A chill passed over his arms, and he rubbed it away. Lee's left ear remained unhearing as always, but a new sound reached his right. There were footsteps on the conservatory stairs. Footsteps, though he could see no one there.

Only, there *was* someone. A blur—not light, like Memory, but dark and earthy, forming into flesh.

Six feet tall, or thereabouts.

Broad shoulders.

And a face.

A man's face.

Lee knew it was him.

"Dad," he whispered.

Vince Vickery flinched and crinkled his brow. He was staring not directly at Lee, but just above him.

"See me," said Lee. "*Please.* See me back."

Vince rubbed his eyes and looked down again, this time straight into Lee's eyes.

"Dad," Lee said.

"*Lee?*"

And then then there was pressure all about him. He was in his father's arms.

"It's happening!" Gretchen cried from the house. "We did it, Felix! Come quick!"

Gretchen and Felix clambered into the conservatory. Lee grabbed his brother by the shirt and dragged him into the embrace.

"It's over," Felix said, wrapping one arm around his brother and one around his father. "No more Agreement."

"It's over!" Lee said, before giving a great *whoop*. He grabbed their hands and, for a moment, he could do nothing but stare at his father's fingers, so large and sturdy and *real*. He grinned up at Vince, and his father grinned back.

Then, with a gasp, Lee pulled away. He felt a rush of bubbling energy, so strong he staggered a step. "Felix," he said, "you've got to meet Mom!"

He led his father and brother into the west end of Poplar House. Felix did not cry out in pain, and Vince did not stop in his tracks, impeded by an invisible wall. Nothing prevented them from crossing the threshold. All three Vickeries set foot in the hallway together, as though it were the most ordinary of events.

"Lee?"

Lee's heart thumped in double time at the sound of his mother's voice.

"Lee, darling, is everything all right?" Judith appeared in the doorway of the kitchen. She wore an apron over her dress and was covered up to the elbows in baking flour. "I was just making . . ."

Judith's words drowned in a deep gasp. She stood frozen, her eyes wide and unbelieving, her hands clenched to fists in her apron. She said, "No."

She whispered, "It isn't possible."

She wiped one hand over her eyes, leaving behind a white, dusty trail.

"Judith."

His father's voice was low and loving—a sound Lee had missed all his life.

"Judith," repeated Vince. He crossed the hallway to where she stood, and he folded her into his arms, and he kissed her. And while Lee knew a normal son would find this rather embarrassing to watch, he did not. For they were not a normal family.

His mother and father held each other for so long Lee began to think they might never let go. And he wasn't sure he wanted them to.

But then his mother's eyes peeked over his father's shoulder, and she cried, "Felix!"

Felix ran to her. Judith crouched and flung her arms around her son, pressing kisses to his hair and neck. She placed both hands on his cheeks, his head, the back of his neck. "It can't be," she said. "It can't be real."

She reached a hand for Lee, beckoning him toward his family, now united after thirteen long, dark years.

"Can it?" Judith whispered, touching Lee's shoulder as though he too might be a ghost.

And it was, it was, it *was* real, and Lee let out the longest, loudest laugh he'd ever laughed.

EPILOGUE

I•I•I

IT WAS THE coldest December in Boone Ridge's recorded history. The *Boone Herald*'s Christmas Eve headline read RECORD LOWS NO MATCH FOR HOLIDAY CHEER. Lee thought it was a wonderful article, because it was so optimistic, and because it ended by wishing everyone in the town happy holidays with their loved ones, and because, for the first time in his life, Lee was spending the holidays with *all* of his loved ones.

Felix had laughed at the title and called it sentimental. Lee hadn't minded that. He'd just been glad to hear Felix *laugh*. More than that, he was glad Felix could sit at a booth with him at Creek Diner on a day other than Halloween, and share a hot chocolate and a town newspaper.

The Vickeries left Poplar House. They sold it to a wealthy state senator who had been searching for a "rustic reprieve" for the months the General Assembly was not in session. The senator had been willing to pay top dollar, and with those top dollars in hand, the Vickeries moved to a little house in town. The house had wide blue shutters and a stone chimney, and, best of all, it was not divided into east and west ends. It was open and airy, with few walls and many windows.

Memory came to live at the Vickeries' new abode, and Judith Vickery continued her profession like before. Now, however, both Lee and Felix helped to bottle the memories, and the work was done far quicker and in far better company. Vince Vickery retired from his career as a doctor. He took up woodworking and in the summer began to travel and sell his wares at local craft fairs. Soon, townspeople were swearing up and down that Vince Vickery crafted the best hickory wood jewelry boxes in all of Tennessee.

A new Death came to live in Boone Ridge. That was the way of things. Life went on, and so did death. Felix did not know where this new Shade lived, nor who his apprentice was. He tried not to think on things like that anymore.

What both Lee and Felix loved most about their post-Agreement life were the winter nights when all four Vickeries huddled in the parlor around a crackling fire. Lee and Felix played games of chess—which Felix always won—and Vince worked on a crossword puzzle, and Judith read a book of essays, just as if they were an exceptionally normal, perfectly boring family. At any given moment, Lee could look up, and he would see his parents sitting side by side. On occasion, he saw his father lean over to whisper something to his mother and, before he was through, place a kiss on her cheek.

No one in Boone Ridge was surprised to hear that Asa Whipple had run away from home over Christmas break. Many, however, were exceedingly surprised when they learned where he had gone. Essie Hasting's mother had taken him in, and people claimed that when you saw the two together at the grocery or the gardening shop, Ms. Hasting treated Asa as though he were her own son. Which, the townsfolk all agreed, was very good for the poor heartbroken woman, though an absolute marvel considering what an unpleasant boy Asa had always been.

Asa did not cease to be unpleasant. He continued to smile all wrongly, and he still got into the occasional fight in the alleys off Hickory Street. But he changed in some ways, too. He took up a keen interest in gardening, of all things, and was often spotted with a purple flower tucked into the breast pocket of his leather jacket. Other times, people saw him on the front porch of the Hasting house, sitting with his sister and talking in such a way that you could almost imagine he was a nice sort of boy.

But nothing was more shocking than when Mayor Whipple himself did the unthinkable and stepped down as mayor of Boone Ridge. On the day he made his announcement, the town residents whispered among themselves about how aged the man looked. How they'd never quite noticed before, but he really *was* getting along in years, and if there was no Whipple old enough to take his place, perhaps it was for the best that the man retire. Really, if you thought about it, it wasn't so unthinkable after all.

The January following that cold December, there was a new addition to the eighth-grade class of Boone Ridge Middle. He was dark-haired and quiet and wore an eyepatch over his right eye, and he soon proved to be the most eager and attentive student at school. He was Lee Vickery's cousin from the north, and he had come to live permanently with the Vickeries in Boone Ridge. His name was Felix.

For his first school paper in English class, Felix was asked to write about what he wanted to be when he grew up. He wrote that when he was younger, he'd thought he would have to carry on the family trade. But then things had changed, and a new world had been opened to him. Now he wanted to be a journalist and work for a big newspaper that wrote important, unsentimental headlines.

The new boy didn't have many friends, but when it came to the two he did have—they were all thick as thieves. The rest of the school called them the Vickery Trio, and even though Gretchen was a Whipple, she didn't mind; she liked being known for something other than her family name.

The Vickery Trio didn't sit at the orange table in the cafeteria, but at one of the perfectly normal green ones. They joked together and laughed together and were often seen at Creek Diner, or occasionally venturing into Poplar Wood. And if you were ever to follow the trio for more than a week, you would more than likely see them walking down to Boone Cemetery, to lay a new bouquet of flowers on the grave of Essie Hasting.

One Saturday evening, deep into summer, two members of the Vickery Trio could be seen together, sitting atop the roof of Boone Ridge High's field house, their legs dangling and their voices hushed.

"Take a look at your future," Gretchen said, spreading her arms toward the high school building before them. "Four years of cruel and unusual punishment, according to Asa."

"We'll be fine," said Lee, smiling.

"Of course we will. I've got you, and even Felix isn't half bad." More softly, Gretchen added, "A Whipple and two Vickeries hanging out. Who would've thought."

"Do you mind?"

"Things change," said Gretchen, shrugging. "Things have already changed. I'm the only Whipple left to do any Rites."

"Will you?"

Gretchen considered Lee's question, folding and unfolding her hands in her lap. "Well, I know I *can* do them now. And someone has to intercede for the town, keep the balance. I just don't know if that someone should be *me*. If so, I'll do it differently. Not the way Dad did it before. Rites for the town only, not for, you know, my endless power and wealth. Or my true love's affection, or whatever."

Lee nodded and said, "Good."

"Good?"

Gretchen turned to Lee, the midsummer moonlight flooding across her black hair and her blood-red lips. Lee swallowed.

"Good."

Slowly, Gretchen smiled.

Slowly, Lee smiled back.

"Gretchen," he said. "Do you want me to kiss you?"

She laughed and said, "What a stupid thing to ask."

And so he did.

A warm wind whipped up Gretchen's hair. The moon spilled its light on the whole of Poplar Wood, and in the dead of night, the town was full of life.

THE END

RITES

LONG MEMORY RITE

Ten hairs—
From family, five,
From good friends, four,
And one from a lover, present or lost,
Woven together and burned

Memory dearest, Memory be near,
Bring your sought assistance here.
Through cloudy night and warm sunlight,
Chisel wrong, and chisel right
On my stone mind, lest I forget.
Let no day pass from this head's net.

SECOND-CHANCE RITE

A pinch of warm sugar
And a sun-kissed leaf,
Stirred in a stagnant pond

May Passion bless this
venture of mine
Though not the first, this second time.
Let not regret cast down my heart—
No ending yet, but one fresh start.

WISHING RITE

Commingled blood,
dropped from a great height

Oh Death! I implore thee, Darkest Shade
To grant me what fate first forbade.
Bestow on me the Wishing Stone,
That makes all hidden mysteries known.
Reveal yourself to summoning eyes,
And give to me the sacred prize.

GUILT RITE

Fresh tears
And fresh blood,
Heated over an open flame
On a moonless night
In an abandoned abode

Your bad deeds will find you like dawn eating night,
Your nightmares will torment your sleep.
Your murder will track you, a wrong seeking right,
Your image will come from the deep.

TRIAL RITE

A memory,
A flower,
A burning candle—
A token from each of the Shades, combined
Heat the memory with the candle's flame,
and add Passion's flower

Now convene, oh mighty Shades,
Whether day or night.
Stand witness two against the one,
For errant deeds must be set right
Till summoning work is done.

ACKNOWLEDGMENTS

All my thanks to Beth Phelan, agent extraordinaire, who rooted for this story from the moment she knew of its existence. My undying gratitude to Taylor Norman, who bowled me over with her support and asked all the important questions, no matter how difficult. Thank you to the Brothers Hilts for creating the perfect haunting-meets-wondrous illustrations. Thank you to Briony Everroad, #GeniusCopyeditor. And a big thank-you to everyone at Chronicle Kids, including Ginee Seo, Melissa Manlove, Amelia Mack, Sally Kim, Lara Starr, Jaime Wong, and others who worked behind the scenes and made meaningful contributions to all my stories' journeys at Chronicle.

Thank you, thank you, thank you to the usual suspects—you know who you are. I wouldn't have been able to tell this story without the love and support of you, my friends and family. PopPop and Nanny Ormsbee, and Granddaddy Ashby—thank you for demonstrating to me what it means to live fully and selflessly. I love you all and miss you every day. Mom and Dad, I'll never forget our weekly read-aloud sessions. Thank you for believing in my stories, just as you've always believed in me. You raised your daughter to question everything; I know Gretchen would approve.